BLOOD CITY

Also by Keith Remer

Killing Bardoe, Book One of The Calamitous Breed Trilogy

The Hiding Place of Thunder

BLOOD CITY

BOOK TWO OF
THE CALAMITOUS BREED
TRILOGY

BY

KEITH REMER

Honey Lee Press
Oklahoma City, OK

This book is a work of fiction. Names, characters, places, and incidents either are products of the author's imagination or are used fictitiously. Any resemblance to actual events or locales or persons, living or dead, is entirely coincidental.

The Calamitous Breed
All rights Reserved

First Honey Lee Press trade paperback edition March 2019
Manufactured in the United States of America
10 9 8 7 6 5 4 3 2 1

Print ISBN 978-0-9998532-2-1
EBook ISBN 978-0-9998532-3-8
Library of Congress Control Number: 2019902412

For my eldest son,

Coy James Remer,

Who grew into a man

I greatly love and respect.

NORTH AND WEST OF TEXAS

1895

CHAPTER ONE

Bad Blood

The gambler paid the liveryman his due and hurriedly attempted to saddle his gelding. Time had come for him to leave the town of Santa Fe in New Mexico Territory and leave it damned quickly. He first noticed the crook-backed little man who boarded his horse turn toward the wide door to the livery stable and then quickly slink away to a far and safe corner of the establishment. Only then did he observe the ominous shadow cast from the sunlight beaming through the wide opening. The gambler jerked his head toward the double-door entry to find it blocked by a man mounted on a sleek and muscular coal black stallion with a long and flowing mane. As if coming out of nowhere, the man and his animal seemingly spewed forth from the very depths of hell.

The rider's tailored clothing matched the black of his stallion's hide. The material of his thigh-length frock coat resembled that of his trousers with the pant legs melding into boot tops nearly reaching the man's knees. Each boot top exhibited an explicitly tooled rendering of a crucifix upon which dangled the tortured body of Christ. Beneath the coat peaked a vest of brocaded velvet and beneath that a sparkling white shirt of satin. A wide gun belt heavily bejeweled with silver and turquoise accompanied the vest and shirt to contrast with the bleakness of the man's dark coat and trousers. Atop his head he wore a low-crowned derby. Two long braids black as midnight protruded from beneath the derby and lay across the front of the man's wide shoulders. The braids and the brownish color of the man's skin revealed his identity.

"I've heard tell of you," the gambler croaked. "You're that Apache Indian. The one they say can't be killed."

The man straddling the snorting and stomping stallion snarled to show bright and well-kept teeth. "And some say I am the devil."

"I won that game back there fair and square," the gambler insisted, anxious to change the subject of the Apache's reputation.

"Of that hand of cards, I have no interest. I was dispatched by a man you cheated north of here Friday last."

The gambler never heard an Indian who could speak the language of white men so eloquently.

"I've not been north of here in the past year," the gambler said without being able to calm his voice or breathing.

"You, sir, are both a liar and a cheat. Alas, I've been paid handsomely to insure you never lie or cheat again."

Before the gambler could offer further debate, the Apache spurred his horse and the stallion bolted forward. The gambler tried to jump aside but could not match the speed of the thundering animal. The stallion reared on his hind legs and his front hooves sliced through the air to strike the gambler to the ground. Dazed and bleeding from the head, the gambler reached inside his coat for a hidden derringer, but the Apache leapt from the horse and moved to stand astraddle him with a nickel-plated Smith and Wesson .44 caliber in each hand. He bent at the waist and firmly pressed the barrel of each into the gambler's eye sockets.

"You will now walk through the valley of the shadow of death," the Apache whispered.

Contrary to the referenced verse, the gambler did there and then fear evil, but he did not fear it long.

* * * *

Laughing Billy Bemo sat on a straw mat in the cool confines of an adobe hut on the outskirts of El Paso, Texas. He worked at cleaning beneath his toenails with a butcher knife while the woman he loved lay next to him sleeping. The Mexican woman named Camilla bore Laughing Billy's unborn child in her large round belly.

The Rangers apparently led their horses in to take up their positions around the hut because Billy did not know they lurked outside until one called his name.

"Laughing Billy Bemo, you murderous crazy son of a bitch!" a harsh voice bellowed. "We know you're in there. Come on out with your hands a showing. There's a noose and gallows waiting on you in Austin."

Billy tossed the knife on the mat while shaking his head and snickering. He then pushed off the mat to crawl on his knees to the nearest window.

"Now how in blue blazes did you bastards ever find me in this place?" he called out in the good-natured tone for which he'd somewhat grown famous.

"That ain't none of your damned business," the harsh voice responded.

"How many are you out there?" Billy sang out.

"There are three of us. Now, come on out of there, Laughing Billy."

"Just three?" Billy laughed out loud. "Why, hell, I've fought three men before and won."

"They weren't Texas Rangers. Now you are trying my patience, boy."

Billy turned his back to the wall beneath the window, leaned back against it and crisscrossed his legs in front of him. Camilla still reclined on the mat, but no longer asleep. She stared at Billy through eyes wide with fright.

"Don't be afraid," he giggled. "I've been in tighter grips than this, but," Billy said as he paused to scratch at his golden colored hair that fell to his shoulders, "I can't for the life of me figure how them Rangers knew I was here. Hell, no one knew my whereabouts but you and I know you wouldn't …"

Billy looked his Camilla square in the eyes as he talked, and she clearly grew more and more frightened with every word he spoke. The truth suddenly hit Billy and it hit him so hard it stung.

"Well, cut my legs off and call me shorty," Billy grinned. "You did it. You turned me in, Camilla."

The woman he loved didn't speak much English, but Billy could tell she understood the meaning of his accusation because she began to shake, and then started crying.

Billy crawled to her and cuddled up close. He turned on his left side and slid his left arm beneath the crook in her neck and pulled her close. "Oh, my sweet Muchacha Bonita," he cooed, not knowing any more Spanish than Camilla did English. "Don't you cry. Crying never does no good."

While he comforted Camilla with his words and caressed her with his left hand, Billy picked up the butcher knife with his right hand and smoothly slit Camilla's throat. While she lay gasping and thrashing, Laughing Billy gathered his clothing and his guns.

Billy preferred Remington revolvers and never went anywhere without all four of them on his person or easily within reach. Billy also preferred buckskins with lots of fringe. It didn't bother him one iota to be one of the few on the prairie still wearing the rugged apparel. Hell, if buckskins still proved good enough for William Frederick Cody, then they damned well proved good enough for Billy Bemo. Besides, with his blond hair, Billy struck a heck of a fine figure in buckskins. Billy liked looking the part of a dashing outlaw, and there stood the reason he carried four Remingtons. Two he carried butt-forward in holsters. The third he always stuck down the front of his wide gun belt and the fourth he tucked beneath the gun belt in the small of his back.

The Ranger with the harsh voice bellowed the whole time it took Billy to get dressed and heeled.

"Aw, hold on to your breeches out there, lawman!" Billy shouted back with a chuckle once he'd moved into place beside the only door to the hut. "Hell, can't you give a man enough time to say goodbye to his wife?"

"We'll give you five more minutes," the Ranger replied.

"I could use ten. Can't you just give me ten minutes of bliss since I'll soon be spending eternity in hell? What you say, Ranger? Can't you give me time for a special kind of goodbye?"

Billy could hear the mumble of voices debating his request. Shortly the harsh voice called back begrudgingly, "We'll give you ten minutes, Laughing Billy, but not a second longer. Best get right to saying your farewells."

Billy stood beside the door for about two minutes, just long enough to let the Rangers settle a bit in their saddles. With a gun in each hand, Billy looked to Camilla who now lay dead as a rock with her eyes wide open.

"Say my farewells?" he giggled aloud to himself. "All right then," he grinned while nodding at his lover's corpse, "Farewell, bitch!"

In the next heartbeat Billy bolted out the door with both guns blazing and laughing his ass off.

As luck would have it, Billy certainly took the Rangers by surprise. One of the Rangers evidently thought ten minutes time enough to crawl out of the saddle to turn his back on the hut and make water. Billy hit that one first, right between the shoulder blades. He died with his rooster still in his hand.

A second Ranger fumbled with his rifle while trying to get a spooked horse under control. Billy emptied one Remington and all but the last round of another before knocking that one out of the saddle.

By now the third Ranger engaged in shooting back. Billy pulled his other two Remingtons as a bullet from the Ranger's Winchester nicked his right hip with just enough bite into his flesh to spin him around and throw him to the ground. Billy dropped one of his last two guns, but still managed a firm grip on the other. From a sitting position with bullets kicking up all around him, Billy took careful aim and blew the last Ranger off the back of his horse.

Only the pissing Ranger died immediately. The other two remained alive, but too badly wounded to do anything but stay conscious. Before Billy picked the best of the three horses and high-tailed to the north, he robbed the dead ranger of his badge and staked the two wounded Rangers out spread-eagle to roast under the scorching heat of the south Texas sun.

* * * *

"I could get to liking this here kind of life, Zeke," Chuck Lawson said as he sat sipping a beer and rocking in a chair on the planked porch in front of the Lone Star Saloon of Beaver City in the strip of unclaimed land surrounded by Kansas and Texas. "Just mosey about all night keeping an eye on them old cows and singing them a song now and again. Then sitting out in the bright sunshine just a rocking in a chair and drinking beer all day. Yup, ol' pard, I might up and tell boss Tackett you and me will just take the midnight watch permanently. What you say about that, Zeke?"

Zeke didn't say a damned thing. He simply shook his tail and stared at his master with the same loyal look he'd displayed over the past ten years of man and dog being best friends.

Lawson lowered his mug and let the huge shepherd take a lap or two. Once the dog removed his thick pink tongue, signaling he consumed enough this round, Lawson took it to his lips and took another hearty sip of the fourth beer they'd shared that morning. It surely looked to be a wonderful day with nearly four beers down and Larson with enough squirreled away from last week's pay to buy at least four more.

Zeke flopped down at Lawson's feet and looked ready for a nap when rough and boisterous laughter erupted from within the thin walls of the saloon situated directly across the unpaved street from the Lone Star Saloon. Zeke jumped to his feet and his ears pointed forward as he looked that direction and started to growl.

"Don't let them peckerwoods rile you, Zeke. If they keep minding they own business, you and me will mind ours as well."

Zeke didn't care a darn bit for the hands who rode for the Four Deuces Ranch. The saloon across the street, the Red Bull, served as their watering hole while the boys of the Tackett Ranch wet their whistles at the Lone Star. Lawson never heard of two outfits getting along so miserably with each other. Cowboys on each side knew the bad blood between the hands stemmed from Ben Tackett's and Stew Graybow's passionate hatred for each other. Graybow owned the Four Deuces ranch, commonly referred to as the Four-Twos. All involved anticipated an out and out range war for the longest time, but as of yet, neither group sinned grievously enough against the other to justify the first battle of the war.

Except for Chuck Lawson, no other cowhand on either side would venture into Beaver City and the perspective saloons all by his lonely. Lawson could do it because he had Zeke to watch his back. Lawson stored confidence in the fact that ol' Zeke, in a scrap, would do as good as any three cowboys he'd ever ridden with.

Zeke settled at the sound of his master's voice and once again plopped down and closed his eyes. Only a minute or two passed before it occurred to Lawson that Zeke presented a whopper of an idea. The conditions certainly invited snoozing. He pushed his feet out in front of him and crossed one boot over the other. He no sooner pulled his stained and crusty hat down over his eyes when the previous night's watch and the four beers put him smooth out.

* * * *

Neither Buzz Libby nor Dan Strapp walked as steady coming out of the Red Bull as they did going in. The bright sunshine made them both wince and groan.

"Mr. Graybow ain't gonna be none too happy with us being drunk in the middle of the day," Strapp commented, wishing now he hadn't let Libby talk him into going in the saloon in the first place. Someday, Strapp vowed, like he had a number of times before, he would give up letting Buzz Libby talk him into doing things he knew weren't right.

"Hell, ain't neither one of us drunk," Libby scowled. "We just a little tipsy. We'll be sober as virgins by the time we make it out to the Four-Twos with that supply wagon."

"At least we picked up the supplies before we got drunk," Strapp replied.

"Tipsy," Libby insisted.

"Graybow would call it drunk," Strapp mumbled.

Libby scrunched his face in concentration, and then nodded his head. "Likely so, but too late to be worrying about that now. You should have thought about that before going into a saloon."

Sometimes Strapp just wanted to haul off and box Buzz Libby's ears, but they'd been partners too long for that to happen.

They both made it off the porch and walked a few paces in the direction of their wagon when Libby reached out and grabbed Strapp by the shirt sleeve.

"Would you look at that?" Libby said while pointing across the street in the direction of the Lone Star Saloon.

Strapp looked and then shrugged his shoulders. "It's just Chuck Lawson and his mean dog."

"Just? Don't the haughtiness of that man gall you in the least little bit? Here in town all by himself, taking a nap in the broad light of day like he ain't got a damned thing in the world to fear."

"It's for sure he ain't got much to fear with that devil by his side. I wouldn't want no dealings with that dog."

"I think the feller needs to be taught some respect for the riders of the Four-Twos," Libby growled.

"Now, Buzz," Strapp hummed.

"Don't 'now, Buzz' me, Dan. Hell, we nearly sworn enemies with them boys and this one is simply thumbing his nose at us. Besides, Stew Graybow wouldn't want us sitting still for this type of behavior."

"Well, you do have a point there," Strapp reluctantly agreed.

"Let's have us a little fun with him, Dan."

Buzz Libby's idea of fun didn't always match Strapp's.

"It might help us sober up a bit as well," Libby added.

"Okay," Strapp sighed, "but I ain't getting' close to that dog."

* * * *

Chuck Lawson could hear Zeke making a ruckus, but it seemed as if Lawson heard the sound from deep within a cave while Zeke remained outside the cave like he'd done a few years back when a hunting party of Comanche cornered both the man and his dog down in west Texas. Back then, Lawson tugged Zeke with him into a cave and held him in place until nightfall. When it grew good and dark, he let Zeke go, and the formidable canine both discouraged and scattered the savages who couldn't see or smell as well in the dark as Zeke could. Lawson bet those Comanche to this day talked about the white man who partnered with the dog as ferocious as a bear. If Lawson had not had Zeke, he would most assuredly not lived to see the sun come up the next morning.

Along with Zeke presently pitching a fit, Lawson could hear a thumping sound of something striking something else all around him. It sounded like plum-sized pieces of ice striking a chuck wagon during a prairie hail storm. Still grappling with sleep, Lawson assumed the sounds were dream generated until one of the thumping things collided with considerable force into his right shoulder. It felt almost as if a tiny fist punched him pretty damned hard. The pain from that punch fully aroused Lawson and caused him to push his hat back from his eyes.

The bright sunlight momentarily blinded him, but his ears now worked just fine, and the intensity of Zeke's barking signaled serious trouble at hand. Lawson's eyes seemed to take their good time recovering from deep sleep and adjusting to the brightness. He could just make out two figures in the middle of the street engaged in some type of activity causing them to do a lot of moving. And the movement clearly corresponded with the thumping sounds of hail hitting something solid. In the very next moment, Lawson deduced that two men in the street were bending to pick up rocks and then winding up to chuck the rocks at both him and his dog. In the very next moment following that moment, one of those two men landed a good-sized rock solidly upside Lawson's head not an inch above his right eye. Lawson reacted instinctively by grabbing his head with both hands and letting out a blood curdling shriek which he immediately wished he'd held inside.

Zeke went hog-assed wild and sprung off the porch to bear down hard on the two rock throwing sons of bitches before Lawson could do a single thing about it. He did try hollering his name, but he barely got it out between his lips when Zeke leapt through the air in the direction of the man to Lawson's left. Although it had been only mere seconds since he'd been rudely awakened from deep sleep, Lawson now knew two things for sure. First thing being that those boys in the street cowboyed for the Four-Twos. Second thing being that one of them now definitely had his teat in a wringer.

For just about a split second, Lawson thought this would prove great fun to watch, although the rock to the head had made his vision even worse. In that minute flash of time, Lawson saw Zeke land on his target and then observed a blur of limbs, legs, fur, and cowboy apparel which immediately resulted in three horrible sounds in quick succession. First came the tortured bellow from a bitten cowboy followed by a gunshot and finally a mournful yelp, which too quickly died away.

Right in front of Chuck Lawson's eyes, his best friend in the whole world just got shot dead. Two immediate options rushed to his groggy, throbbing, and awfully grief-stricken mind. Lawson could either break down into tears or he could strike out in vengeance. So, he did both.

* * * *

When the dog came off the porch, Dan Strapp nearly shat his jean pants. He probably would have done it anyway had the beast not set his muzzle for Buzz Libby. Strapp considered Libby about as good a friend as he ever had, but he'd be lying if he said he didn't feel a great deal of relief when the dog chose Libby instead of him, which seemed only right since Libby concocted the idea of throwing rocks like a couple of school boys.

Strapp earned only a few pounding heartbeats to look back and forth from Libby's torn and bloody arm to the dead dog lying in the street. When Chuck Lawson started to wail, Strapp wondered how in the hell he'd ever missed the fact that nothing but ugly could come out of throwing rocks at a sleeping man with a mean-assed dog dozing at his feet.

Strapp could not recall ever hearing a grown man crying out loud in public. So quite naturally, the sound of such caused him to look up immediately. When he did, Lawson already had his gun out and started the process of pointing and thumbing back the hammer. Strapp did not immediately go for his gun. Up to the here and now, not a single cowboy from either the Four-Twos or the Tackett Ranch had thrown lead at one another. They all believed it inevitable, but Strapp never thought it would start over thrown rocks and a dead dog. Of course, Strapp considered himself a common-sense kind of man and plain old common-sense dictated you didn't steal another man's woman and you damned sure best not harm his dog either. Strapp also didn't go for his gun because Lawson stood a good thirty paces away and Strapp considered himself an up-close kind of shooter. Libby, on the other hand, could shoot pretty well, but he shot with his right hand, and his right arm currently hung torn and limp along the side of his body. Besides all that, Strapp had seen plenty of men pull a gun plenty of times but never once pull a trigger. It seemed possible Lawson could be just that kind of man.

However, that quickly turned out not to be the case. He did in fact pull the trigger. Because he did, Strapp recognized no option other than pulling his gun and shooting back. Out of the corner of his eyes he could see Libby struggling to grab his gun with his left hand from the holster on his right hip. In the next instance, all three men sent lead flying as quickly as possible. Dirt kicked up and wood splintered from nearby structures as smoke and dust filled the air, but Lawson counted as no better shot than Strapp, and Libby shown not worth a damn with his left hand. In a matter of seconds, eighteen bullets flew in all directions and soon three hammers clicked as they fell upon spent shells.

Libby could be considered the only true shootist in the group because he dry-fired only twice before he tucked his gun between his knees and started a fumbling effort to reload with the only good hand he had. Lawson decided on another tactic. He jumped from the porch, reared back, and gave his empty gun a mighty fling in Libby's direction. It turned out Chuck Lawson threw much better than he shot. His heavy old Colt Navy landed with a sickening thump against the bridge of Libby's nose. Strapp became so enthralled with the way Libby spun and fell that it shocked him to look up and see Lawson bearing down on him in a dead run with tears just a streaming.

Strapp packed a gun for many years but he'd never until now participated in what the dime novels coined as a "shoot-out." But he'd gone fist to fist more times than he cared to count and considered himself much better at scrapping than shooting. It also didn't hurt being at least six inches taller than Lawson and out weighing him by a good twenty pounds.

The considerable size advantage, to Strapp's dismay, did not prevent Lawson from plowing into him like a twister and riding him to the ground. Because of his momentum, Lawson ended up on top and promptly found Strapp's neck with both his hands. Lawson not only choked Strapp, but used the powerful grip on his neck to raise and lower Strapp's head in a whip-lash motion that caused his head to pop against the hard-packed dirt road. Strapp started throwing punches into the smaller man's midsection, but they seemed to have no effect.

In a different situation, Strapp might have thought it funny that his thoughts suddenly turned to an old boy he once knew who owned a foot-tall monkey. For money, that old boy would pitch the monkey against any man's fighting cock, tom cat, or dog - up to medium sizes. Strapp never saw anything fight with the ferocity of that little monkey. Until now. Truth be told, Lawson at the moment presented Strapp with a monkey kind of whipping.

When the bright light of day started to fade in Lawson's eyes, he switched from punching to trying to dislodge the hands around his neck. He about gave up all hope until he caught sight of Libby suddenly looming over Lawson's back. Libby held his pistol in hammer fashion and began to pound on the back of Lawson's head with the butt end of the pistol. It took more blows than Strapp thought probable, but Lawson finally sagged, and Strapp managed to roll from beneath him.

While Strapp struggled to his feet, Libby, with blood spraying in all directions from his ruined nose, viciously engaged in kicking and stomping Lawson. Because the man now on the ground had nearly choked him to death, Strapp felt justified to lend his own boots to the endeavor.

* * * *

At the sound of the first shot being fired, Elijah Smith dove behind the counter of his nearby dry goods store and then hollered for his wife, Margaret, to do the same. As had been her way since the first day of their marriage only a year earlier, Margaret did as she damned well pleased. She moved to the nearby store-front window to get a glimpse of the gun play. Elijah had of lately begun to think the two primary curses of his life were building his store next to the Red Bull Saloon and marrying an independent kind of woman well past the prime marrying age. Margaret Binder had most assuredly been the prettiest woman in the region, and still was, but she ended up being just too much woman for Elijah Smith to handle.

A whole passel of other shots rang out, and Elijah heard two bullets smack against the outer cedar planks of his store. He thought the shots striking the building would send Margaret scurrying, but not that woman. She stood right there at the window insisting Elijah take some action other than hiding behind his counter.

When the firing stopped, there existed a relative calm outside the walls of the Smith store, but within the walls Margaret wailed.

"Elijah! Two men are kicking and stomping a man lying on the street. They're surely going to kill him. Get up from behind that counter and go to his aid."

Elijah intended to do no such thing and told his loving bride exactly that. Then he heard the sound of their front door being pulled open.

"If you won't, I certainly will," Margaret called on her way out the door.

Elijah hunkered down even lower and cradled his head in his hands.

* * * *

Strapp continued in a stomping frenzy until he heard the female voice call out from off to his left.

"Stop that! Stop it now, for the love of Christ! You're going to kill that poor man!"

The sound of the shrill voice brought reason back to Strapp's thinking, somewhat anyway. Libby stopped kicking as well, but spun on the woman.

"Lady, you best carry your arse back in that store, or I'll carry it back in there for you." He even started in her direction. The woman started backing away, not so much to get away from the approaching cowboy, but more so because the kicking and stomping ceased.

Strapp returned wholly to his senses, due more to Libby's intended action with the woman than with the condition of the man lying in the street. He reached out to grab a handful of his friend's shirt.

"Buzz, we've done enough harm for one day. Let's end this foolishness right now."

For once in his stubborn life, Libby paid heed to a voice of reason. He paused for long seconds to take heaving breaths of air through his mouth. His fractured nose could certainly not do the job. Strapp bent to rest his hands on his knees and recovered his breath as well.

"Oh, hell," Libby finally managed while pointing to the ground just a few feet away, "what are we going to do with those two?"

"Let's find his horse and lash him to it. The horse will find its way back to the Tackett ranch," Strapp offered.

Once they tied the unconscious and badly beaten man to his horse, Strapp and Libby put the body of Lawson's dog up there with him.

Strapp applied a hand to the horse's rump to send the mare off in a trot.

"What if he dies before he gets there?" Libby asked.

Strapp took a minute to think before finally responding, "Then you and me, old pard, will have started something we will surely live to regret."

* * * *

Dick Thurman owned a livery stable on each end of town, but maintained an office in the one on the north end. Dick heard the gunfire from a chair behind his desk and knew he would soon be welcoming visitors. Not that those coming would be all that welcome. Being the elected mayor of Beaver City, Thurman considered it a thankless job.

Tom Johnson out ran the other merchants to be the first to burst into his office. All the rest soon followed. Thurman tossed the dime novel he'd been trying to enjoy upon his desk.

The town's business owners babbled in excited voices all at one time. Thurman pieced together from all the noise that the boys from the Four-Twos and the Tackett ranch had been at it again. But this time the fracas escalated into shooting and grievous harm fell upon one unnamed ranch hand. Some insisted the cowboy assuredly died from a most vicious beating.

"And my blamed wife," Elijah Smith's voice protested above the rest, "thinks me cowardly because I refused to throw my body in the mix."

Several in attendance raised an eyebrow to the confession. It just proved the fact that no man should marry a woman manlier than he could ever hope to be.

"We've known all along it would one day come to this," Tom Johnson shouted above the din. "We need a lawman in this town!"

"We have no law for a lawman to enforce," Thurman shouted back.

The stated truth created a hullabaloo, which Thurman expected. A chorus of voices bellowed the complaints Thurman heard all too many times, of which he could not disagree with a word spoken.

"Our families and businesses are in danger!"

"We can't safely walk the streets in the light of day, much less at night!"

"Stew Graybow and Ben Tackett run this blasted town!"

"We're plagued with whores, gamblers, drovers, and outlaws that come up from Texas and down from Kansas!"

"We need to make our own damned laws!"

"We voted you mayor. Do something!"

Dick Thurman jumped up from his chair and banged his fists on the desk until the hubbub slowly dwindled to near silence.

"If I've told you once, I've told you a dozen times, you all will have to put your money on the table. It will cost a great sum to hire the kind of lawman needed to clean up Beaver City. I'll throw in five hundred dollars, but it will take the same from each of you."

"Five hundred dollars?" the voices cried in unison.

"I don't make much over that in most years' time!" Elijah Smith bellowed while all the others agreed with "Me either!" or "Here-here!" or "Amen, brother!"

"Yeah, but you have all made it in the past, and might not make it in the future if we don't put it up now. Besides, you all have at least that much in Charlie Mann's bank."

Charlie Mann stood present and offered nothing to the contrary.

"So, it comes to this, gentlemen," Thurman said solemnly. "Put up or shut up. I'm darned tired of being your whipping boy."

Several minutes of grumbling followed, signaling individual contemplation on funds held in reserve.

Finally, Blake Moore, the innkeeper, spoke up. "If we were to come up with that kind of money, I guess you have a man in mind for the job?"

"I most certainly do," Thurman grinned as he reached out and grabbed the dime novel off his desk. He then held it at arm's length and slowly moved it to and fro so all could see the name and likeness printed on the front cover.

"Why in the world would he come to Beaver City?" banker Charlie Mann questioned.

"For the money, of course," Thurman returned. "And if not for the money, then for the opportunity to have yet more books printed about the ways and means he used to free our fair city from the grips of the lawless hordes."

There followed yet more minutes of grumbling, but with a noticeable reduction in hopelessness.

Elijah Smith stepped up front and center and thumped the picture on the front of the dime novel. "If you can get him to come here, I'll put up my share of the money."

It took a while, but soon all agreed to the same.

CHAPTER TWO

Hiring A Gun Hand

Long and forceful strides carried Ben Tackett across the barnyard and into the bunkhouse. All the while he spouted cuss words causing even Moose Powell to wince. Powell served as Tackett's foreman, and they called him Moose because he came close to being just that big. Ward Avants and Shannon Wheeler, two of the ranch hands who worked beneath Powell, found Chuck Lawson about a mile away from the ranch headquarters and on the north bank of the Beaver River.

"I thought you said he was alive," Tackett bellowed.

"He is alive, boss," Powell commented.

"He damned sure looks dead."

"No, sir. Look close and you'll see his chest moving a little every once in a while."

Moose studied the ranch owner's face while Tackett stared down at the terribly bloodied and unconscious Chuck Lawson. No cactus grew rougher than Ben Tackett and the rancher would never admit it in words, but Moose could see in the old man's eyes he lamented over Lawson's dreadful condition. Tackett had the reputation of a hard man to work for, but if he cared enough to let you work for him, he took you in as one of his own.

"Do we know who did this?" Tackett mumbled.

"No, but we're betting…" Moose started.

"I know what you'd be betting, but I don't want nobody jumping to conclusions. I'll ride into Beaver City and see what I can learn."

"Me or one of the other boys will ride with you," Moose nodded.

"Don't need nobody to ride with me. I pity any fool toying with me between here and there."

Moose nodded his understanding and agreement. Moose had yet to fight the man he could not whip. But, he'd never fought Ben Tackett and he never would. Mostly out of respect, and the rest out of fear. The much smaller Tackett bordered on being elderly, but many considered him one of the two toughest men in those parts. The other man, Stew Graybow, owned the Four-

Twos. The two old bulls had grown damn tough wrestling their pieces of the world out of the grip of the Comanche.

"Have you sent for Missus Gale?" Tackett asked.

"Yes, sir. I sent Zed. He should be at the Gale place by now."

Old Lady Gale provided comfort as a nurse in the War Between the States and currently served as the closest thing to a doctor within a hundred-mile radius of the Tackett ranch. If Zed Martin had made it to her home, he'd be another hour getting her back. Moose would not bet Chuck Lawson had an hour left in him.

Tackett inhaled a deep breath and turned away from his downed cowboy. His eyes fell on the stiffening body of Zeke the shepherd.

"They killed his damned dog?"

"Yes, sir. He was strapped up on the horse with Chuck."

Ben Tackett's face twisted into a scowl more pronounced than what he normally wore. "It takes the sorriest kind of son of bitch to kill a man's dog."

* * * *

Dan Strapp stood with his hat in his hand listening as Buzz Libby told Stew Graybow exactly, misstep after misstep, what had occurred in Beaver City with Chuck Lawson and his dog Zeke. A man didn't have to work long for Graybow to know you didn't dare steal from him, and you damned sure didn't tell him no lies.

Graybow carefully listened without interrupting. Once Libby said all he could say, the old man sat silently behind a grand desk in his home office and stroked a long and snow-white beard.

"Exactly how much of a hurt did you boys do to that cowboy?" he finally asked in the calmest of manners.

The boss could throw a fit with the intensity of a prairie thunder storm, but he'd never thrown one in Strapp's direction, and he damned sure never wanted him to. Strapp often thought the world would be an easier place to navigate if every man wore a sign around his neck professing his temperament. He often thought Graybow's sign would read, "I'm not a man you want to make angry."

Libby cleared his throat before responding. "We are not sure he lived long enough to make it to the Beaver River."

Graybow stroked his beard a few seconds longer before nodding his head a couple of times. A few more terribly long seconds passed for Strapp before the boss said, "This is the roughest and toughest of lands. If an ol' boy can't live through a good stomping, he shouldn't have been here in the first place. Strapp, you need to unload those supplies. Libby, you need to get your nose and arm tended to."

Strapp and Libby left quickly to do as told, but Strapp could not hold his mouth shut a moment longer.

"How you feeling about what we did today?" he growled at Libby.

Libby pursed his lips and gave the question considerable thought before saying, "What we did is already done."

It was done okay, Strapp agreed, but he deeply wished it'd been done a lot differently.

* * * *

Ben Tackett made his way back to his ranch and rode about halfway between there and Beaver City when he saw the rider on the horizon coming his way at a gallop. Tackett pulled his Winchester from the scabbard and rested the butt against his upper thigh with the barrel pointed to the heavens. It frustrated Tackett how close a man had to come nowadays before he could recognize him. He'd once been eagle-eyed, but those days were long past. It turned out to be Zed Martin on the horse, but he had to draw dangerously close before Tackett knew that for sure. Tackett took some comfort in knowing, had Martin been a hostile, he'd been shooting long before he rode into the older man's eye-balling range. Tackett didn't have to see a man clearly to knock him out of a saddle at a fair distance. He'd just point to the center of the blur and squeeze the trigger. His eyes might be gone, but his hands were still as steady as any man he knew.

Martin reined a roan mare to a halt and both man and beast took moments to catch their breaths. Martin and his horse were soaked with sweat.

"You've done a fair piece of hard riding today, son," Tackett said as a greeting to one of his most personable hands.

"Yes, sir. That is a fact, and I am now the bearer of just terrible news."

Tackett didn't have to make any guesses as to the nature of the news, but he waited for the younger man to go ahead and say what he'd ridden so hard to say.

"It's Chuck Lawson, Mr. Tackett. He's done gone and died."

Tackett sighed long and hard as he slid his Winchester back into the scabbard. He then took a second to scan the wide-open terrain of sagebrush, sand dunes, and tall grasses. Tackett never kept count of the good men he'd buried beneath the surface of this harsh land over the fifty years he'd been here. Keeping such a running total would have turned a sane man in the other direction.

Although he could not call a number and even though many of the names had faded from his memory, Tackett did know, with the exception of very few, the dead died for some purpose which made varying degrees of sense. The ranch owner had by now talked to enough witnesses in Beaver City to know there had been no purpose whatsoever in the acts resulting in Chuck Lawson's death.

"Well, young Zed," Tackett began when he finally felt like commenting, "I do appreciate you riding so hard to bring me this news, but you do know, don't you, that you could have walked your horse, saving wear and tear on you both, and by the time you reached me I'd been just a little bit closer to home and ol' Chuck Lawson would have been no less dead."

Martin pulled a floppy and battered hat from his head to rub at a mop of sweaty hair. At the same time, he twisted his lips into a near pucker and studied the horizon. After a few seconds of his obvious contemplation, he looked back to Tackett.

"Mr. Tackett, I'm pretty near sure there's a lesson to be learned in what you just said, but for the life of me, I ain't grasping it."

Tackett took the opportunity to chuckle. "Just as well, Zed. It's not a lesson you can't live without."

Martin let go with a wide grin as if relieved to know he missed nothing of grand importance.

"Now, Zed, I want you to listen carefully because I'm going to tell you exactly what happened to Chuck and I want you to go back and tell Moose."

"You won't be riding back with me, boss?" Martin asked.

"No, I won't be riding back with you. I'll be riding back in later on."

The revelation seemed to concern Martin, but he didn't question Tackett further and sat and listened intently as Tackett told what had happened to Martin's friend and co-worker. The older man could see a fire building ever hotter in the young man's eyes as the telling built to the climax. When Tackett finished, Martin first spit and then asked his question through gritted teeth.

"What we gonna to do about them boys, boss?"

"Well, Zed, you are going to let me worry about that. As a matter of fact, I'll be leaving you now to pay Stew Graybow and the Four-Twos a little visit."

"I'll be damned if I won't be right by your side," Martin said shooting up arrow-straight in his saddle.

"No. You're taking what I just told you back to Moose and the others."

"Boss, I ain't never came even close to disobeying your orders, but," Martin started saying with shakes of his head.

"And this ain't no time to begin doing so. You'll head on back to the ranch like I told you to, Zed," Tackett said sternly.

It took Zed a few seconds, but he started nodding his head instead of shaking it. "Yes, sir," he mumbled.

"You also tell Moose to sit tight and keep the hands at the ranch until I return."

Martin chewed on the words for a second or two before asking, "And what if you don't return?"

"The chances are greater that I will rather than I won't. But if I don't, then someone else will be deciding what to do next."

Martin nodded his acceptance of his orders, but Tackett could see in the man's eyes he felt damned concerned. Tackett had learned over the years few characteristics in a man could be more valuable than plain old loyalty.

Before reining his horse toward the east, Tackett looked at Martin and grinned. "Zed?"

"Yes, sir?"

"Keep her at a trot."

"Yes, sir."

* * * *

Ben Tackett started spotting out riders from the Four-Twos about a mile away from the ranch headquarters. By the time he reached the ranch house, four of them followed him at a respectable, and for their own sake, safe distance. Another must have ridden ahead because Stew Graybow stood on his front porch awaiting Tackett's arrival.

"You got more balls than brains, Ben Tackett," Graybow called out. "What the hell are you doing on my land?"

Tackett rode up as close as he could to the porch, which put him less than twelve feet from Graybow. "I think you know why I'm here."

"Yeah, I guess I do." Beneath all the shaggy white hair around Graybow's mouth, Tackett could see lips curling into a cruel smile. "But I don't know what you thought coming here would do for you."

"Chuck Lawson was a dependable hand and a damned good man, and now he's dead," Tackett said while trying to keep an even temperament. He'd learned many years earlier, if a man let his lips and tongue get too hot, they'd melt away a cool head in a hurry.

Tackett waited for some sign Graybow might actually give a damn about a man being dead. When no such sign came, Tackett garnered no surprise and continued. "I've come here to get the men that killed him. Been told they are Buzz Libby and Dan Strapp."

"Get 'em in which way?" Graybow chuckled. "You going to fight me and all these boys to get at 'em?" he asked while making a sweeping motion with his hands to clearly make sure the surrounded Tackett realized as much.

"I'd hoped to come here and take them away with me," Tackett said, struggling mightily to keep a cool and calm head.

"If I was to let you have them, which, of course, I won't, what did you intend to do with them?"

Now Tackett showed a mean little smile of his own. "I intended to hang the sons of bitches!"

"You knew I wouldn't hand over my men to you, and you took a hell of a chance coming here. You have no guarantees we won't do to you what was done to Lawson," Graybow growled.

Tackett keyed his horse with rein and spur to slowly begin to spin in place. As the horse turned, Tackett called out to the four cowboys who, although not crowding him, had him corralled. "Which one of you boys is going to step on up to pull me off this horse?"

Tackett didn't expect a response and he didn't get one. Graybow waited until Tackett once again faced him before he said his piece.

"All I got to do is say the word, and they'd be stepping up."

Tackett lowered his voice to say words he wanted only Stew Graybow to hear. "I'm not so sure they would be, and neither are you. We both know you are the only bastard here mean or tough enough to try taking me out of the saddle. And I bet your chances are about equally good to either fail or succeed. But if you was to fail, your cowboys would have a front seat viewing of your failure. That'd be somewhat embarrassing."

Graybow just glared at Tackett for so long Tackett began to think the other old man just might make a run at him. He hoped it didn't show, but he grew more than a little relieved when Graybow opened his mouth to speak.

"Have you got anything else to say before you get off my land?"

"Yup, I do. I knew you wouldn't turn those boys over to me. And I don't see them standing around here, but if they don't already know it, they'll know soon enough that I rode in here all by myself just looking for them. They'll know by that alone the kind of trouble they are facing."

Tackett reined his horse around and started off in a slow walk.

"Ben Tackett!" Graybow called after him.

Tackett turned in his saddle to look back, but didn't stop his horse.

"One of these days before I grow too old to do so, I'm going to kill you dead."

Tackett turned back in his saddle without batting an eye or offering a single word of response. Stew Graybow had been threatening to kill him for thirty or so years now. The threat had long ago lost its sting.

* * * *

It fell well past dark when Tackett made it back to his ranch. Late enough that there normally would be no signs of human life lurking about the grounds, but coal oil lamps still burned in the bunkhouse, and Tackett could make out a few forms rocking in the chairs on the long and low porch in front of the bunkhouse. At the far end of the porch, he caught a glimpse of the glowing tip of a cigarette. Then the place really came alive when someone announced his arrival in the form of a joyous shout. In a matter of seconds, five cowboys crowded around Tackett's horse and they expressed, to a man, their delight he made it back safe and sound.

Moose Powell's booming voice quieted the others when he asked, "Is Buzz Libby and Dan Strapp still walking among the living?"

"I didn't get the privilege of laying as much as an eye ball on those bastards," Tackett called down from his horse. He would have dismounted, but his hands didn't afford him enough room to swing a leg out of the saddle. "But I did get the message delivered that they'd be paying for their crimes."

"We gonna to ride on the Four-Twos, boss?" the very lanky and terribly bowlegged Shannon Wheeler asked from his place beside Tackett's right stirrup.

"Shannon, just yesterday Graybow had seven cowhands, and I had six. He still has seven, and now I have five. I don't like those odds."

"Hell, Mr. Tackett," Zed Martin said in taking his turn, "any one of us is equal to any two of them rascals."

"Zed, I'm the very first to agree that my boys are huckleberries above them persimmons, but I lost one of you today, and I don't care to lose more tomorrow or any other day to follow. And I'm pretty damned sure Chuck Lawson wouldn't want a single one of you dying for his sake."

"I've rode for you for a heck of a long time now, Mr. Tackett," Dick Avants spoke up. "And I think I know you well enough to bet you ain't gonna to let Chuck's death go unavenged."

"Oh, they going to get what's coming to them, Dick. I'm just not going to ask you boys to bloody your hands or get yourselves killed in doing something others are better suited to do."

"What others would you be referring to, boss?" Kyle Caldwell asked.

"Why hell, boys, we live in a land crawling with the mean and murdering types. There ain't a week goes by some man don't pass through Beaver City that is well qualified to hunt down and take care of Libby and Strapp."

"You talking about hiring a gun hand?" Moose asked.

"I'm talking about hiring an assassin," Tackett nodded emphatically.

Tackett's hands fell silent for a few seconds as they digested the rancher's words and meaning. Zed Martin asked the last question, "But what if one of us was to stumble across Strapp and Libby first? Would you have a problem with us killing them?"

"Well, Zed, if one or both of them ol' boys ain't smart enough to keep their distance from any one of us, hell, we'd be obliged to shoot them down right where they stand."

With those words, the cowboys of Tackett's ranch headed off to bed, seemingly satisfied there would be an adequate repaying for the two bodies they'd be placing in one grave the following morning.

CHAPTER THREE

Done Did It

Any morning CB Wooly wasn't out and about the Oklahoma Territory chasing some outlaw, he could be found having his breakfast at the same place and same time every single day in the Territory's very young capital city. What he ate might change from one morning to the next, but when he lingered in Guthrie, he always took his breakfast at seven a.m. in the restaurant and bar inside the Browne Hotel. Since he'd become so widely known, he always sat where he had a clear view of the door, and seldom did his eyes stray from that critical point. Now that he'd been immortalized in four dime novels, the deputy U.S. marshal's day to day living had grown ten times more dangerous than it'd ever been before.

On this day, Wooly chose two eggs over easy with bacon and a couple of biscuits with Missus Browne's famed gravy. He sipped at hot and strong coffee and looked over the brim of the cup to see a slight man in gentleman's garb come through the door. Wooly summed in a matter of moments the man offered no threat, and he felt no need to ready a weapon as the stranger approached his table.

Before the man spoke a word, Wooly could tell by the nervous look on his face that all he knew of CB Wooly, he'd read in one or all of the dime novels.

"Excuse me for intruding, Marshal Wooly, but may I have a moment of your time?"

Wooly set down his cup, leaned back in his chair, and graced the man with a smile. "You don't look like the type to be seeking infamy, so you must be a reporter."

"I'm neither a glory seeker nor a scrivener," the man smiled back. "I'm the mayor of Beaver City."

Wooly pointed to a chair, "Well then, pull up a seat and take a load off, Your Honor."

* * * *

Dick Thurman's pounding heart slowed the very moment CB Wooly gave him a smile, and his breathing became easier once offered a chair at the famous gunman's table. The sound of Wooly's voice sounded just as the novels had touted, a rich and easy-going baritone. It surprised Thurman though that Wooly seemed larger than the picture painted in his mind by the written word, and older too than Thurman expected, but not elderly by any means. Thurman had expected a man in his prime, but Wooly looked just a tad past prime. There grew more gray than black in the well-trimmed mustache and goatee, but the lively green eyes danced with an energy one author described as "constantly capable of turning terribly violent." Thurman could see the butt end of one walnut pistol grip peeking from beneath the stylish gray top coat, and he could not help but be in awe of what might be the very gun that ended the life of the infamous Clay Bardoe. The Boss of the Plains styled hat Wooly preferred rested on its flat crown next to a plate of bacon and eggs that appeared barely molested.

"I apologize for interrupting your breakfast, Marshal," Thurman commented as he nodded toward the plate, relieved his words now came somewhat easier.

"Believe me, Your Honor, my breakfast has often of late known much more demanding interruptions. Do you care to join me? I highly recommend Missus Browne's flap jacks if you've never had the pleasure."

"Please, sir, my name is Dick Thurman, and I prefer you calling me Dick. Thanks all the same, but my innards aren't up for breakfast."

The famous man seemed to find that funny and chuckled in a good-natured sort of way. "Okay, Dick, glad to meet you. I prefer being addressed as CB."

With that, CB Wooly offered his hand and Thurman gave it a hard and vigorous grip which Wooly returned in kind. Thurman believed a man could speak volumes with the manner in which he shook hands. He passed far from disappointed with what CB Wooly's grip had to say.

"So, let's just jump right to it, Dick. What brings you to Guthrie and my breakfast table?"

Thurman, too, liked a man who didn't dally on getting right to the point. "CB, we're in a terrible fix in Beaver City. We have no laws, and if we did, we have no lawman capable of enforcing them. We are being overrun by rowdies and no accounts and two feuding clans of cowboys from neighboring ranches."

Wooly chuckled yet again. "Well, Dick, Beaver City is deep in the heart of No-Man's-Land. I wouldn't expect to hear any less."

"CB, we prefer the region be referred to as the Cimarron Territory, but the United States Congress has so far been less than accommodating."

"That's what I read in the newspapers, Dick," Wooly nodded.

"In that, you are informed correctly," Thurman said before taking a deep breath. "Would you have any interest whatsoever in bringing law and order to No-Man's-Land? And if not, could an interest be spurred with a promise of a salary equaling four times a year what you make as a deputy U.S. marshal?"

For just about a fraction of a second, Thurman thought he captured Wooly's undivided attention, but then those lively green eyes darted up and focused on a point beyond Thurman's back. Then they narrowed and took on a glare instantly producing a chill. Almost simultaneously a shrill voice rang out from behind Thurman.

"CB Wooly! I've come here to put you in your grave!"

Wooly's eyes never flinched from their target, but the man quickly bent to the right and his corresponding hand darted to the floor. When it came back up, it wielded an oak axe handle with no iron axe blade on the end. In an instant, Wooly jumped up from his chair and hurried past Thurman's place at the table.

Thurman jerked around in his chair to see a young man, barely beyond his teens, poised with a hand on a still holstered revolver. Wooly bore down on the man with his oak club at the ready, and the younger man had the look of one who could not decide if he should pull and shoot or simply shit his drawers. Thurman barely had time to draw a breath before Wooly brought up the club and then swung it mightily to connect with a sickening thud against the elbow above the hand gripping the still holstered weapon.

That arm and hand went limp as Wooly pulled back the club for yet another blow. The next one crashed into the young man's other elbow and produced the same crippling effect. The want-to-be assassin yelped in pain and swayed on his booted feet only a heartbeat or two before a third strike from the axe handle landed on his forehead and knocked him to the varnished floor. The man twitched a few times and then went smooth out.

Wooly shook his head as he gazed down upon the assailant. Then he turned to look toward the bar and the burly barkeep who maintained it. "Ben, would you do me a favor and drag this tom cat to the alley?"

"I'd be privileged, Marshal," Ben nodded enthusiastically.

Thurman got the impression such had become a routine for the barkeep named Ben.

CB Wooly returned to the table, plopped down in his chair and sighed heavily as he placed the club back on the floor next to his right foot. "Dick, as ugly as that might have been, I've learned in the year and half since killing Bardoe, I could save both a load

of bullets and a passel of worthless lives by simply breaking a few bones."

More now than ever before, Dick Thurman felt convinced CB Wooly could indeed be the one man capable of taming Beaver City.

* * * *

Wooly hadn't lost his appetite for his bacon and eggs. It would have taken killing the would-be assassin to accomplish that, but the runny yolk had congealed and the bacon grown cold. He pushed the plate aside and leaned back to consider the man across the table as well as the offer he'd put upon the table. Dick Thurman expressed consideration by not interrupting Wooly's silent contemplation. Wooly held in high esteem any man with that kind of common sense and manners.

"Dick, at least once a week, I deal with a breed of riff raff as I just knocked out cold. About half the time, I hunt them down as part of my sworn duties. The other half, they hunt me up because they want to make a name for themselves."

Ben, the barkeep, had just refilled Wooly's cup with steaming coffee, and Wooly took a break to thank him and take a sip. "To be just down right honest with you, Dick, I'm growing weary of long days in the saddle as well as busting elbows and breaking heads. Just recently I've given consideration to retiring and traveling back east to Richmond to live in my ancestral home I inherited upon the death of my dear and sweet old mama." Wooly at this point could not keep from showing embarrassment in a smile he offered Thurman. "Truth is, though, I simply have not stuck back enough money to do so."

Wooly paused for another sip of coffee and to give Dick Thurman an opening to make any comments. The man proved patient and wise enough simply to keep his mouth shut and wait for Wooly to conclude his point. Wooly had a great respect for patience, and he did not often have the privilege of dealing with a man of wisdom.

"I'm sure some folks think I made a heap of money by letting that old boy write those silly stories about me. The fact is they cost me much more in aggravation than they ever paid me in coin. So now, Dick, I've said all that to say this, I'd truly appreciate making four times what I'm presently paid for preserving law and order. And in my advanced age, walking in and about a town appeals more to me than riding an entire territory. Mayor Thurman, you've hired yourself a lawman."

Wooly could tell by the expression on Thurman's face the man from Beaver City had not anticipated such an easy sale. The two men shook hands again and both grinned broadly while doing so.

"Dick, I'm going to need a set of laws to enforce. Have you given that any consideration?"

"I have, CB. We had a council make proposed laws as part of the process in our bid for territorial status. We didn't win over Congress, but we got laws on paper."

"They'll work just fine. We'll also need a judge or a justice of the peace. As the mayor of the city, you could fill that role just fine and dandy."

"Well now, CB, I'm just a simple livery man. I've never studied law so I'm certainly no lawyer."

"Good. I've never met a lawyer that wasn't about as useless as stepped-in dog shit. Do you have a jail?"

"Don't have a jail, but we'll get to building one."

"Good, we're going to need a jail. Won't need gallows, we'll just use a nearby tree when we have to string one up."

"That could be a problem, CB. There are few trees out that way and especially no good-sized ones. It'd take a very short and skinny criminal that could hang in one of our kind of trees. Now,

I do own livery stables. We can suspend the condemned from the rafters of one of my barns."

"That'll do! Have we about covered all that needs covering, Dick?"

"You didn't make mention of needing deputies, but I'm prepared to provide you two, each making one half of what we pay you."

"Well, that's certainly generous, but on the spur-of-the-moment, I don't have anyone in mind for the positions. Yet, I seem to draw newspaper reporters like a wound draws flies. I'll have them put out the word that I'm looking for two good men."

"I guess that just about does it, CB. The only remaining question is, well, when can you start?"

"I'll need two weeks to tie up my business here."

Dick Thurman stood and extended his hand for the third time. "I'll see you in about two and a half weeks, Marshal Wooly."

Wooly stood and again accepted the hand of friendship. "Mayor, unless some loco son of a bitch happens to get lucky, I'll be there."

* * * *

Moose Powell stood out in front of the Red Bull Saloon with one fist clenched and the other wrapped around a near empty whiskey bottle.

"I know you're in there, damn it! There's two horses tied up out here with the Four-Twos' brand on their rumps. Now, I'm going to call you out one more time. Then I'm coming in to get you. I'd rather do this right out here in the middle of the street, but if I have to destroy the inside of that skunk den, then so be it."

Five days dwindled away since Chuck Lawson passed, and Powell grew angrier and meaner day by dwindling day. Lawson had been one hell of a hand and a damned close friend. Powell would bet what little he owned that, next to Zeke, Lawson would have considered Powell his best all-around partner. Now he lay dead and buried and for a whole five days not a damned thing had been done about it. It wasn't Friday just yet, but Powell stewed long enough and slipped away to town in the early afternoon hoping for just this very opportunity. With any luck at all, the two riders inside the Red Bull would be Buzz Libby and Dan Strapp. But if not those two, Powell prepared to settle with whatever two he could get his hands on.

Powell passed the bottle from his right hand to his left and then used his right to remove his old pistol from the holster. He then bent and laid the gun on the street.

"I'm not heeled now, boys. I've just placed my iron in the dirt. It's just me and my two fists. I don't intend to kill you unless you are Libby and Strapp. If that's who you are, I'm going to beat you both to death just like you did my friend Chuck Lawson. If you are anybody else, I just figure on hurting you real awfully bad."

* * * *

Bill Norris and Lester Jiggs stood side by side at the bar in the Red Bull. Both stared intently at the door. Norris felt as if he'd swallowed soured milk.

"That statement don't make me feel no better," he said without averting his eyes from the door.

"Me neither," Jiggs nodded.

The bellowing man outside had not identified himself, but Norris knew the voice belonged to the foreman of the Tackett ranch, Moose Powell. And he knew Jiggs knew it as well. They also knew if it came to fisticuffs, Moose would indeed hurt them both real awfully bad.

"He said he's not armed. We could just run out and shoot him," Jiggs offered as a solution.

Norris shook his head. "I ain't never killed a man, but I've seen what Buzz and Dan have been reduced to. Neither of them boys been worth a durn for the past week. Killin' must make good men feel really low."

"Yeah, you right," Jiggs agreed, "I ain't in a killing mood either. Maybe we could just wing him."

"It'd be like winging a grizzly," Norris mumbled.

The bartender and owner of the Red Bull, Marvin Little, stood across the bar from the two cowpunchers. "I don't know what to tell you boys, but if that mean son of a bitch tears my place up, I'll hold you two accountable."

Norris quickly came up with an idea. "Marvin, you could lend us a hand. With three against one we might stand a chance."

"Ain't my fight," Marvin returned. "Besides us three against Moose Powell ain't odds I'd be willing to bet on."

Jiggs then came up with the best words Norris figured he could. "Damn, I wished I'd just stayed at the Four-Twos this afternoon."

It fell clearly upon Norris to get them out of this jam. It took him long minutes, but he came up with a plan. Norris walked within a safe distance of the door and hollered out to the street. "Moose Powell, can you count to a hundred?"

It took a second or two for an answer to be returned. "I ain't sure. Why you ask?"

Norris felt a tinge of relief. "Because we need that long to decide how to best fight you. We're trying to decide if we should come out one at a time or both all at once," he hollered back.

"I'll count as high as I can," Powell answered.

* * * *

Moose Powell made it through only the third grade and couldn't even write his own name. Educated or not, though, he considered himself a fair kind of man. Powell started to count, but not out loud. He didn't want himself embarrassed if the numbers got too high to manage.

It finally got to a point where he couldn't for the life of him remember what followed seventy-nine. So, Powell just stood outside for what he thought might be a hundred numbers worth of time.

"Okay, you stink assed varmints, get on out here!" he finally bellowed when he grew tired of waiting. "I've done counted to a hundred, and I ain't counting no higher."

Powell had never been comfortable with lying, but sometimes the truth simply conflicted with convenience. To make amends for the lie, he waited longer than he thought reasonable for the two men to show themselves.

"Okay, you have given me no other choice. I'm coming in there to give you your whooping."

Powell stomped upon the front porch and barreled right through the front door of the Red Bull Saloon to find it empty except for the owner, Marvin Little. For a moment or two he felt stumped.

"Who was in here and where the hell did they go?"

"Bill Norris and Lester Jiggs is who," Little blurted. "And they done scurried out the back way."

Before the news could sink in deep, Powell heard two excited voices outside giving commands for horses to move out quickly. He then heard the beating of hooves responding to the commands.

Moose turned an ugly glare on Marvin Little. "I think I'll just give you their whooping."

Little bent below the bar and came up with a double-barreled shotgun he laid across the bar. Both barrels pointed directly at Moose Powell's broad midsection.

"I thought you might think that," Little grinned, "but I suggest you rethink it."

Moose paused and, before turning to go, mumbled, "I done did it."

* * * *

Dan Strapp looked up to see Buzz Libby headed his way. Mr. Graybow kept them both pretty close to headquarters since Ben Tackett paid his visit. Graybow seemed to take damn serious Tackett's ability to see that Strapp and Libby paid for killing Chuck Lawson. On this afternoon Strapp shod horses in the cool of the barn while Libby replaced busted or rotten corral poles out beneath the rays of the glaring sun.

Libby, soaking wet from sweat, walked into the coolness of the barn. Strapp's back ached a little, but he sure preferred the job he'd been given over the one Libby drew.

"Damnit, Dan, are you going to stay sore at me forever?"

Strapp thought about his answer as he let go of a freshly clipped hoof and straightened to stretch his back. "Hell, Buzz, I'm sorer with myself than I am with you. Long as I've known you, you ain't once twisted my arm to make me go along with one of your piss-stupid ideas."

Libby grinned sheepishly and shrugged his shoulders.

"But you are still a bad influence."

Libby grabbed the rolled end of a battered hat and pulled it from his head to wipe at a broad and sweaty forehead with his shirt sleeve. "Yeah, I know that's the truth."

"Buzz, did you have even an inkling of an idea that what we planned would result in a man being dead?"

Libby's face scrunched in what looked like discomfort. "Nope. None whatsoever. Heck fire, Dan, I know I ain't admitted it until now, but I feel damned bad about Lawson being dead. If I had it to do all over, I'd left the man to his afternoon nap."

"Me too," Strapp nodded. "Yeah, I surely would."

"You know I killed another man one time up in Topeka. But he was a terrible mean son of a bitch and he was coming after me with a knife. I never felt bad about shooting him dead. But this time, well, it's different."

"You think Ben Tackett and his boys are really and truly going to make sure we pay for what we did, Buzz?"

Libby wiped at his brow again before pulling his hat back down on his head. "Oh, hell, Dan, you know how it is. Tempers flare, but then they eventually cool. I think they're probably already considering letting bygones be bygones."

Strapp pondered the possibility and hoped for Libby to be right when they both heard the ruckus of riders coming in hard and fast. Both men stepped out of the barn to see Bill Norris and Lester Jiggs reining winded horses to a halt.

"Wild Indians after you boys?" Libby jokingly called out to them.

"Worse than that," Jiggs hollered down from his saddle. "Moose Powell might just be following us in."

"Moose Powell?" Strapp questioned. "Hell, Moose ain't going to ride up in here."

"I don't know," Norris responded. "He's damned sure all riled up. He cornered us in the Red Bull and said he was going to hurt us in a bad way. We had to run out the back to get away from him."

"Moose could damn sure hurt a man real bad," Libby agreed.

"Hell, Moose Powell would have killed you both," Strapp added.

"Nope. He threw his gun in the street. He was just going to whip us real good… or bad," Norris said. "Now, if we'd been you two… he said he would kill us."

Strapp scowled at Libby, "Moose must not be one to let bygones be bygones."

"I got to get back to mending those fences," Libby said as he turned and stomped away.

"We both have some fence mending to do," Strapp called after him.

CHAPTER FOUR

A Killer Of Men

CB Wooly reminded himself for at least the tenth time since striking out for Beaver City that any man in his right mind wouldn't ride through Stillwater to get from Guthrie to No-Man's-Land. Again though, he yet reminded himself, a man in his right mind might not be making the trip to Beaver City in the first place. The risks involved in the new job Wooly accepted seemed considerable to say the least. For that reason, he felt compelled to make a stop in Stillwater. It struck him all too likely that he might not make it back this way again.

He'd left two hours before sunup and the sun would soon be sinking beyond the horizon. It'd been a hard day's ride and Wooly felt every mile of it as he climbed out of the saddle and hitched his buckskin gelding to the little fence encircling the remote spot of land on a small hill just outside Stillwater.

Wooly stood idly by and scratched the horse between the ears as he considered the place and why he'd come here. "I won't be long, Moonshine," he said soothingly to the horse he had, in a sense, adopted.

Wooly stepped through the white-washed gate and maneuvered around the assortment of wooden and rock uprights until he stood facing side by side graves. Wooly removed his hat and smiled down on the mounds of earth.

"Good evening, Millie," he nodded to the grave on the right.

He took a deep and cleansing breath as he turned his eyes to the grave on the left. "Howdy, Clay."

He studied the single slab of granite marking both places of rest. Large letters pronounced the infamous name BARDOE. Beneath that smaller letters identified the names of husband and wife, Clay and Millicent. A final line of script professed, "Together Once More to Never Again be Apart." Wooly had chosen those words and his money provided the tombstone for the best man he'd ever known, and the woman the man loved more than life itself. The large hunk of granite served as a monument to the man Wooly had been forced to kill.

Books had now been written on the murderous spree prompted by Millie's awful death and carried out at the hands of a man who took extraordinary measures in his distant past to shoot but never kill. In much earlier days, Clay Bardoe had been CB Wooly's partner and the most capable deputy U.S. marshal with whom Wooly ever rode. Had Clay Bardoe gotten his way, he would have lived out his days as the store clerk he'd later become, loving his magnificent Millie, and living a peaceful existence. As fate would have it, Bardoe would forever be recorded in the annals of history as the most vicious and cold-blooded murderer to ever live in these parts. He brutally killed five men and even a woman who got in his way, and then Wooly had been forced to kill Bardoe.

The dime novelists called it a "gun battle" and a "shoot out." As the only living witness, Wooly solely possessed the truth that the novelists had it wrong. He'd never told any who interviewed him anything but the truth. He just never told the complete truth. As a result of all that had been written, Wooly's notoriety matched that of such proclaimed greats as Wild Bill Hickok and the Earp brothers. This certainly would not have been the case had Wooly ever provided a key fact that played hell with his conscience to this very day. A key fact that, had it not existed, CB Wooly would most certainly now be the one lying in a grave.

"The only difference being, old pard," Wooly now thought out loud, "is that I'd been laid out all by my lonesome. I envy the fact, Clay, that you found that one special love. If I've missed anything in life, it's been just that, the love of a good and special woman."

Wooly had to take a very deep breath and rapidly blink his eyes to clear them. "I guess the only thing that now keeps me from going out of my mind, the only thing that allows me to look at my face in a mirror, is the fact that I provided what you most wanted. I sent you to be with your Millicent."

Wooly placed his hat back on his head and cleared his throat. "Well, Clay, I just came to say so-long, ol' pard. I'm headed out west where there's some hellions making life rough on good citizens. Those good citizens are expecting me to be able to take on all comers. The baddest of the bad and the meanest of the mean. Because I'm the man that bested Clay Bardoe."

Despite himself, Wooly couldn't help but chuckle before adding, "Ain't that a kick in the ass?"

CB Wooly stood and silently studied the graves for just minutes more before tipping the brim of his hat and walking away.

* * * *

Near bedtime Margaret Smith placed the four thin paperback novels on the counter in front of her husband. "It is done, Elijah. I did as you asked and read the books Dick Thurman provided."

Her husband's normally bland expression grew optimistic. "Do you feel differently now about CB Wooly coming here?"

"Not at all." Margaret often wished she possessed the skills that allowed others to more gently express the truth, but as a born and bred product of No-Man's-Land, she'd grown hopelessly blunt. "If anything, I'm now more concerned than ever before. This CB Wooly is a killer. He may very well wear a badge, but he is a killer of men."

"Margaret, how can I convince you of the necessity of bringing him to our town?"

"The only necessity I see, Elijah, is for the men of this town to start acting like men."

"I am not a gunman, Margaret. I have never worn a gun and neither have three quarters of the other businessmen in Beaver City."

"The cowboys from the Tackett and Four Deuces ranches wear guns, Elijah, but they are far from being gunmen. It would not take what those pathetic little books refer to as a 'shootist' to settle them down. It would simply take the men of this town taking the matter in hand and forcing them from our town, or forcing them to behave when they are in our town."

"Those cowboys are not the sole source of our problem, Margaret. What do we do about the truly bad element that comes in all too often from Kansas and Texas? For those types, we need a man like CB Wooly."

Margaret nearly progressed to the point of raising her voice. She took a moment to calm herself, not because she felt any wifely duty to show respect to her husband, but because when she did raise her voice, Elijah wilted like a flower in the heat of summer. She did not need any further reminders of the type of man with whom she errantly promised to spend the rest of her life. Margaret's father, John Binder, had been one of the city's founding fathers. He'd been one of the many men who had fought bloody battles to take and hold this land from the Comanche. It was damningly difficult for Margaret to deal with a man who did not know how to act like a man.

After long and deep breaths, Margaret said calmly, "If anything, Elijah, a man like CB Wooly will attract other deadly men if for no other reason than to shoot him down and claim his fame as their own. Heed my words, there will be blood in our streets like we have never seen before. We might as well, right this instance, change the name of our town from Beaver City to Blood City."

* * * *

The judge awoke with an uneasy feeling of not being alone in his rented room. He rolled to his side and reached to fumble in the dark for matches on the bedside table. After locating them and getting one to strike, he applied it to the wick of the coal oil lamp resting on the tabletop. As the lamp flickered to life, the judge shielded his eyes with a hand in order to let them adjust to the sudden illumination. When he dropped his hand, he gasped and flinched at the sight of the figure of a man occupying a wing-backed chair in a corner not five feet from the bed. The man wore black from the well-shaped derby on the top of his head to the stove top boots practically reaching his knees. The man in black appeared comfortable in the chair with his hands resting calmly on the padded arms and one leg crossed casually over the other. His head was cocked to the side and, from that perspective, he studied the judge. The dark skin of the intruder along with thick braids lying across the front of his shoulders marked him as a blamed Indian. The judge's response changed from fear to indignation.

"How dare you, savage! Do you have any idea who I am?"

The Indian's expression remained impassive and his demeanor calm as mud, but his answer came immediately. "I know you are a judge appointed by none other than the President of the United States to travel in a circuit throughout the Territory of New Mexico. So, therefore, yes, I know you are a circuit judge."

The judge curled his lips and pointed his nose high, "Although I cannot imagine why anyone wasted their time and effort, you are obviously an educated Indian. Therefore, you must certainly understand you are trespassing in the room and disturbing the peace of a very powerful man."

The Indian snorted in obvious contempt. "Outside the walls of a courthouse, few are more impressed with the status of a judge than a judge himself. Here and now, I am the only one in this room that possesses any power whatsoever."

The judge felt his face flush with anger. "Who are you and what business have you here?"

The Indian nonchalantly brought his arms off the chair and crossed them loosely over his wide chest. "I go by many names. There is the name my people gave me before I was taken from them at a very young age by Catholic missionaries. And, of course, there is my Christian name given to me by the Catholics upon my confirmation in their faith. Although, most priests I now encounter call me Diabolos. Mostly though, I go by names I've given myself."

The judge shot upright from beneath his bedding and swung his legs off the side of the bed. "Mister, I've grown tired of this intrusion and I demand…"

Very suddenly the judge found himself staring down the nickel-plated barrel of a very large handgun. His words stopped coming, but his mouth still hung open.

"You will demand nothing in my presence. You are a rude and pompous little bastard. Open your mouth one more time without me asking you to do so, and hell almighty will sweep down upon you right here in this very room. Now, where was I?"

The judge had been a man of great importance so long he'd forgotten how it felt to be inferior to anyone, but now he remembered. This *Indian* had suddenly gained the upper hand and now dominated the judge with stark terror. The judge cleared his throat and breathed deeply, but still his voice came out sounding fearful. "The names you gave yourself?"

"Oh, yes, thank you. Sometimes I call myself Michael and other times I call myself Samael, for I most certainly must be an Archangel. It's just that I can never truly be sure if I am the Good Angel of Death, Michael, or the Evil Angel of Death, Samael."

"An angel of death?"

"Most certainly."

For the first time ever, the judge empathized with the many he had condemned. "Who sent you?"

"Sometime back you took one thousand dollars to find an innocent boy guilty of raping a rich man's daughter. You knew all along no rape had occurred, but you said the words and the boy did, indeed, hang by his neck until he was dead. That poor boy's father now wishes that you should die as well."

The Indian, who the judge now chose to think of as Diabolos, stood, reached in his coat with his free hand and came out with yet another nickel-plated revolver. The judge's eyes started to sink to the floor but fell upon the richly embossed crucifixes on the front of each shiny black boot. Two Christs were suspended bloody and dead.

"Now you witness my dilemma," Diabolos said. "You are a hypocrite and a murderer. By killing you, am I performing a good task or an evil one?"

He did not wait for an answer, but stepped up close and stuck the revolver's painfully deep into the judge's eye sockets. The judge began to shudder and his breathing became difficult, but he listened intently to the words practically whispered in his ears.

"Judge not, that ye be not shot through the head."

The circuit judge carried those words into eternity.

* * * *

Laughing Billy Bemo rode the dead ranger's horse up to the front door of the little sod house. He had carefully watched for, but had not spotted any homesteaders. He sat on the horse watching the house for a minute or two before shouting out a greeting.

"Hello there! Anybody in the soddie?"

He waited and had nearly drawn a conclusion the simple structure housed no occupants. Then the door slowly opened and a young face framed with blonde hair peeked out.

"My husband is in the fields, but keeps a close eye on this house. He'll be here any minute now," the woman said.

"Now ain't no call in acting all skeer'd," Bemo chuckled. "Can't you see this badge on my buckskins? Hell, young lady, I'm a Texas Ranger."

"What you doing here?" The woman asked as she took a cautious step onto the porch.

"Well, I might just be looking for the prettiest little darling in all these parts, and I might just have found her," Bemo said with a laugh.

The woman blushed, but she did not in the least look offended. "My husband will be here shortly," she said with a coy smile playing at the corner of her full lips.

"You love him?" Bemo teased.

"He's my husband," the woman blushed again and averted her eyes.

"Don't mean you love him. Lots of wives don't love their husbands."

"You're a bold one," she all but giggled.

"If you wasn't expectin' him to be here so soon, could I have given you a little tickle, or maybe gotten a kiss?"

Her lips didn't say yes and her eyes didn't say no. Bemo neared the point of insisting on a kiss and maybe even more when an agitated voice called from off to the side of the house.

"Who the hell are you and what the hell you want here?"

Bemo looked in the direction of the voice just as a man in bibbed overalls stepped around the corner. He looked much older than the woman and stood unarmed except for the spade he held upright in his right hand.

Bemo grinned easily and nodded. "I'm a by God Texas Ranger, that's who I am. And I stopped to find out if I've reached No-Man's-Land yet."

"A by God Texas Ranger ought to know if he's still in Texas or not," the man scowled.

"Texas is a big state," Bemo laughed. "Lots of people don't know where she starts and where she ends. Now, I'll ask again, am I in No-Man's-Land yet?"

The farmer pointed the tip of his shovel toward the north. "Nope. It's still another two days' ride that way."

"Now, was that so hard?" Bemo chuckled.

"You got further business here?" The farmer grunted.

"Well, it'd be awfully neighborly of you to offer me a bite to eat, me bein' a Ranger and all."

The man glared at Bemo for long moments before turning the same mean glare at the blonde on the porch. "Fix us both something to eat, woman. Don't make it much, and don't take long about doing it."

Before darting back in the sod house, the woman shot Bemo a sassy glance signifying to Bemo she felt mighty pleased he'd be staying a while.

Bemo turned back to the farmer with a smile plastered all over his face. "Hell, ain't no sense in you and me standin' out here in the heat when we could be sittin' at the table in the coolness of your soddie."

The farmer stepped upon the porch and invited Bemo to follow him into the house with a nod of his head. The two men weren't seated at the table, but a moment, before the woman set before them each a cup of coffee. Every opportunity Bemo could get without being caught he'd steal a glance at the fine-looking woman. Every time he did, she was stealing one of him as well. It wasn't long at all before she put a bowl of beans and a slab of cornbread in front of her husband. She went back to the stove to get the same for Bemo and when she brought it back to the table, she did so in a manner to block from her husband's view the ankle she extended from beneath her day dress to rub against Bemo's calf muscle.

Bemo all but swallowed his food whole and finished eating well ahead of the woman's husband. So, he reached and grabbed his most convenient Remington and pointed it across the table at the man's chest.

"Mr. Farmer, I hate to interrupt your dinner, but I'm going to have to ask you to step outside. I've taken a cotton to your fetching wife and intend to have my way with her!"

The woman let out what seemed a very unconvincing gasp and the old man bellowed.

"You ain't no damned Texas Ranger!" He said with bean juice dripping off the whisker stubble on his chin.

"You are not a man to be hornswoggled, are you?" Bemo mocked with laughter before saying, "You got it right. I ain't no ranger. They call me Laughing Billy Bemo, and I am a killer of men. I killed three rangers just a short while back." Bemo slapped the badge with his free hand. "I got this off one of them, and that horse out there off another. Now, Mr. Farmer, I find killing right before fornicating seems to dull the pleasure of both. But, I will not now ask you a second time to step outside."

The husband never turned his eyes off Bemo to even look in remorse at his wife, who seemed much engaged in fighting off a giggle. Without uttering another word, the man pushed up from the table, grabbed what remained of his beans and cornbread and stomped out of the sod house. It occurred to Bemo, if it had been in him to do so, he might have felt sorrow for the man's predicament.

The woman barred the door behind her husband before turning complete attention on her guest. She was not shy, and she went about a carnal pursuit like a bird denied the ability to fly. Bemo sensed the older man had not been sufficiently performing his household tasks. Not that many minutes later, Bemo pulled back on his buckskins.

The woman lay naked on the floor and looked up at Billy with a smile still on her lips. "If you don't kill him, then he will kill me."

Bemo threw back his head and laughed before replying, "You should have thought about that before serving up the quim."

"You might someday want to come back for a second helping. If I'm dead, you won't get none," the woman aptly pointed out.

"You'll be here if I come back?" Bemo grinned.

"Only if I'm not in the grave. I ain't got no place else to go."

"I ain't going to bury him," Bemo he-hawed.

"I know how to dig a hole."

Bemo unbarred the door, jerked it open and pulled a gun for each hand. The husband slumped on a nearby stump with the bean bowl at his face giving it a final licking. Bemo showed his appreciation for the hospitality and said his farewell by emptying both Remingtons into various parts of the farmer's body.

CHAPTER FIVE

Damned Good at It

The best CB Wooly could figure the town posted a sentry who spotted him at a distance and rode in ahead to announce his arrival. Mostly men lined the main street, but also a good number of women and children were on hand, all of whom certainly had to be the core of Beaver City's respectable citizenry. What waited didn't by any means qualify as a celebration, but more a gathering of the curious who produced as a by-product their welcoming nods, waves, and smiles. A few of the men even stepped out into the street and offered up their hands for shaking.

Although the gathering resulted in little fanfare, it still sparked more attention than Wooly cared for. He never participated in grandstanding and his skills at such now allowed him to do no more than return each nod, wave, smile, or handshake with a duplication of the offered gesture. Wooly particularly experienced a great deal of unease when one man with a woman in tow stepped up awfully close to Moonshine. Maybe the horse simply sensed his rider's discomfort, or maybe the horse was no fonder of attention than Wooly. Either way, it took more effort than usual to keep Moonshine under control. All of Wooly's thoughts and effort turned immediately to doing just that, until he caught the slightest glimpse of eyes as brilliantly green as the spring fescue blooming back in his home state of Virginia. Captured by that mere glimpse, Wooly turned his complete attention to the face of the woman standing next to her man, and he'd never, not in all his years, not in all his travels, ever seen a face so beautiful. The hair worn in a tight bun over the magnificent face glowed as fiery red as most assuredly were the flames suddenly igniting Wooly's chest.

* * * *

Margaret had not been given the chance to protest. She stood alongside her husband and watched CB Wooly approach on horseback. Suddenly, Elijah grabbed her hand and tugged her into the street.

"We should make him feel welcomed," Elijah said as he pulled her toward the oncoming horse.

It seemed all too obvious that Elijah wanted Margaret to be wrong about CB Wooly. If she proved wrong, and Wooly could and would do more good for the town than harm, then Elijah would never have to worry about her prodding him again to take a manly stance. If Elijah and Dick Thurman were correct in their summation of the man, then neither those two or any other Beaver City civic leader would ever have to take any courageous stands. They'd have CB Wooly to do it for them.

Margaret had only seconds before being jerked into the street to get a good look at the new lawman. She immediately picked up on Wooly's downright embarrassment by the turnout of people wanting a peek at their newest and immediately most prominent citizen. She did not detect a lick of the brashness the dime novels depicted. Strangely, Margaret thought he appeared simply too demure for his physical size and deadly reputation.

Elijah had been too enthusiastic about meeting Wooly and practically threw both himself and Margaret beneath the hooves of the very big horse. Atop the horse, a man more mature in his years and better looking than Margaret expected, spoke kind and respectful words to his animal having an immediate calming effect. Margaret got only brief moments to marvel at the man's gentle demeanor before their eyes locked for a period of time too fleet to count even in seconds, but not so swift Margaret failed to recognize the look of a man instantly and magically smitten.

Though she adamantly attempted to deny it, she too experienced a fluttering in her chest no respectable wife should have to endure.

* * * *

CB Wooly settled into a rented room Dick Thurman secured in the boarding house. It was early evening, normally too early for Wooly to turn in, but the days of travel and the strain of the one-man parade had taken a toll. Especially taxing had been the plunge he took into those magnificently green eyes. By now, the encounter had played over and over in his head and the best he could explain, because he'd never experienced anything remotely powerful, it felt like he'd been captured, tortured, and then tossed aside to suffer.

Had he been free to do so, Wooly would have, at the moment of the encounter, clicked his tongue at Moonshine and rode like hell to the far end of the main street. Initially though, he succumbed to a near trance-like state of awe. Then the man beside the beauty extended his hand while making introductions. As a result, Wooly stumbled headlong into captivity, and for a man who never allowed himself to be captured, he did not know how best to deal with the state of helplessness which he therein found himself wallowing.

Now in his quarters, Wooly could not repeat the names because he'd been unable to pay attention to the words coming from the man's mouth. At the time of the introductions, his mind had not yet returned from the place his eyes had taken him. Wooly did shake the man's hand. Then the woman pushed her right hand up toward him as well. Wooly stared at the hand because he simply could not again look her in the face. At the time, it seemed like miles his hand had to travel to connect with hers. The touch of the hand felt like heaven. Letting go of it hurt like hell.

Wooly removed a bottle of sour mash whiskey from the scant belongings he'd transferred to his new life. Since killing Bardoe, only this elixir allowed him to sleep through the night. He sipped nearly a half of his first glass of the whiskey before it occurred to him the imagined distance from his hand to the woman's extended hand surely represented the long years he'd traversed before finding the woman who could move him in the ways this woman had so effortlessly done. The irony of such did not evade him. This long-awaited treasure was not free for the taking. She was not free at all.

Wooly took the bottle and glass to the unfamiliar bed. Tonight, he would not only have to drink to dull the vivid memories of killing a best friend, but also to erase from his heart's memory the face and wondrous touch of a woman who had already found her life's mate.

*　*　*　*

Moose Powell gave Zed Martin and Shannon Wheeler the afternoon off, and both high-tailed it to Beaver City and the Lone Star Saloon. All the men out at the ranch already knew CB Wooly was coming to Beaver City, but they didn't know what Martin and Wheeler had just learned from the proprietor of the Lone Star. The famous lawman had arrived the day before.

Just last week Martin managed to lay his hands on two of the small books written about Wooly. Martin couldn't read a lick, but fellow ranch hand Ward Avants could, and he read both books to the other cowboys over the course of three evenings. None of the boys were at all thrilled over law coming to Beaver City, but they were all pretty impressed over the man intending to bring it. Kyle Caldwell said he just planned to stay out of the man's way, but Martin hoped for a chance to meet him. A friendly and unofficial chance.

"Have you gotten an up-close look at him, Don?" Martin asked the Lone Star's owner, Don Stroud.

"I stood right out there on my porch and he passed within three feet of me," Stroud nodded. "That's about as close up as one man needs to get to another, unless it's an awfully cold night and blankets are scarce."

"What's he look like?" Wheeler asked.

"He's a good-sized ol' boy. Not too flashy, but he has some chin whiskers kind of like Bill Cody's sporting nowadays. Wears one of those black Boss of the Plains hat like the Earp boys are said to prefer. He's a serious enough looking man, but I guess he better be. And he rides one hell of a fine horse."

"Could you see any iron on him?" Martin asked. The first chance he got to meet the man, he intended to just out and out ask him if he could hold the gun that killed Clay Bardoe.

"Nope. He had a long coat on," Stroud said as he poured the boys some whiskey.

Martin and Wheeler brought their glasses to their lips at the same time the saloon's swinging doors suddenly creaked the announcement of a new arrival. The door stood adjacent to the bar and Martin turned his head in that direction while peering over the rim of his glass. The whiskey had barely touched his tongue but he tipped his wrist to stop the flow. Martin had been in enough rough and tumble places in his life to know it damned sure looked like trouble just strolled through the door. Anytime any man wore as many pistols as this man did, Martin knew you could bet your ass the pistols had everything to do with what that man did for a living.

The stranger wore buckskins, which wasn't all that common any more, but Martin didn't figure he should be pointing that out to the man. A light-colored hat with a tall open crown and the brim rolled up in front topped the man's head. Long, golden hair fell from beneath the hat and nearly touched his shoulders.

Martin didn't openly stare. He just stole glimpses. A man didn't stay alive out west as long as Martin without having the sense to recognize the types you best not stare at. This man most definitely resembled one of those types. For reasons Martin could not readily explain, he found it unsettling the newcomer, for no apparent reason, had a grin plastered on his face. He looked to Martin like a man who had heard a funny joke he just couldn't shake from his head.

* * * *

Laughing Billy Bemo rode into this town named Beaver City with the intention of finding the nearest saloon. When he found one, he found two, and they were situated across the street from each other. The one on Bemo's right had two horses tethered out front. The other had none. When Bemo drank in pubic, he liked company. Bemo could always have more fun when there was someone near for him to toy with.

There were only three men in the bar, the bartender behind the bar, and two fellers standing before the bar, who obviously owned the horses tied out front. These men's chaps, leather wrist cuffs, and filthy misshapen and floppy hats betrayed their occupation as wranglers. They both wore sidearms, but these cowboys' guns, unlike Bemo's, were worn primarily for protection from harm normally coming their way on either four legs, or slithering on its belly.

Bemo moved to the bar about ten or so feet up-wood from the cowboys. The bartender, a man with a pock-marked face and fairly slender body supporting an impressively round and protruding gut, wasted no time in getting right to Bemo.

"What will you be having, Mister?"

"You got corn whiskey?" Bemo smiled broadly.

Like most people tended to do, the bartender smiled back. "I got corn and rye."

"Bring me a bottle of the corn whiskey, fine sir," Bemo laughed.

The cowboy closest to Bemo displayed about average height and weight with no physical characteristics that allowed him to stand out in a crowd. This one had a friendly, easy going look about him. The cowboy next to the regular kind of man stood tall and skinny and as bowlegged as an upside-down U. He looked to be the nervous type.

Now that Bemo revealed himself as the jovial and friendly sort, the closest cowboy began to be less careful about stealing glances Bemo's way. As a matter of fact, he started getting practically bold about looking in Bemo's direction.

Bemo took a healthy gulp of his first glass of whiskey before squaring around and looking directly at the regular looking man. "Do you think I'm pretty?" He grinned.

The cowboy's response did not come quick or without a fair bit of stammering. "Uh, no."

"Are you saying I'm ugly?"

"Uh, no. I ain't saying that neither."

"Then what are you saying?"

A longer pause and even more stammering came forthwith. "Well, hell, Mister, I don't know what exactly it is I am saying!"

Bemo threw his head back and laughed so hard he had to reach down and slap a thigh. "Barkeep!" He hollered through his laughter, "I'm buying these boys' next round of whiskey."

"Thanks, Mister," the closest cowboy grinned.

The bow-legged cowboy stepped around his friend, "Yeah, thanks, Mister."

Always feeling ornery, Bemo pointed to this one's legs. "How you even walk on them limbs, feller? Hell, from your gut down you're shaped like a horseshoe!"

The man stared down at his legs like he'd never even noticed. He looked up with a shy smile on his thin face. "Well, I ride my horse most places I go."

Bemo let out another howl of laughter. "You two wranglers are all right in my book. A man's got to be able to laugh if he's going to drink with me. My name is Bemo, but you boys can call me Laughing Billy."

"You do laugh a lot," the regular looking man nodded.

"That I do. You two got names?"

"I'm Zed Martin," the closest man said, and then hitched a thumb at the other, "and this is Shannon Wheeler."

"I'm Don Stroud," the barkeeper chimed in, "I own this place. Welcome to the Lone Star Saloon, Laughing Billy."

Bemo shook hands with his three new acquaintances. "Fine place you got here, Don," he chuckled.

The three customers took a moment to gulp some of their whiskey.

"I'm betting you're here to see our new marshal, CB Wooly," Martin said after wiping at his mouth with a shirt sleeve.

Bemo had no idea what the man meant by that, but he never believed in expressing ignorance if it could be avoided. "You reckon?" he grinned at Martin.

"Sure enough. Wooly's looking to hire two deputies. You're packing serious iron. I reckon you might be planning to land one of those positions," Martin grinned back. He then went on to tell what he knew of CB Wooly and how he had killed Clay Bardoe, the lawman turned murderer.

Bemo listened to it all before saying, "Nope. I ain't here to be no man's deputy. I already got a badge." Bemo lifted the lapel of his buckskin jacket to expose the badge pinned beneath.

Martin looked close and then exclaimed, "Damn! You are a Texas Ranger?"

"Nope," Bemo chuckled. "Just got a badge. Truth is boys, I ain't got much use for the law. If you must know, I'm a hired killer, and I'm damned good at it."

Bemo watched with amusement as the cowboys gave each other a serious kind of look. When they turned back to look at Bemo, it surprised him that their eyes revealed an interest instead of dread.

"Laughing Billy, are you currently looking for employment?" Martin asked.

"Why you ask, Zed?" Bemo laughed, "You fellers looking to have someone killed?"

"Well, we ain't, but our boss is."

Bemo listened and sipped his whiskey as Zed Martin told him a story about a dead man and his equally dead dog.

CHAPTER SIX

Reunion

CB Wooly pulled up a chair and watched the workmen applying their skills to the roughed in structure soon to be Wooly's office and jail. The opening did not yet have a door and the form of the city mayor suddenly filled the open space.

"Why, howdy, Dick," Wooly nodded without getting up.

"Good afternoon, CB," Dick Thurman said with a noticeable edge to his voice.

Wooly studied the man's face a moment before stating his deduction. "This ain't no social call, is it, Dick?"

"No, sir. Your services just might be needed, CB."

Wooly listened as Thurman described the man he'd seen entering the Lone Star Saloon. Once Thurman said all he had to say, Wooly shook his head while considering the information.

"Sounds like the unsavory type to me, Dick. I think I'll mosey on over to the Lone Star and make my presence known."

"The Lone Star's the watering hole for the boys from the Tackett ranch, CB. A couple of the cowboys' ponies are tied up out front."

Wooly gave that a few seconds of thought as well. "It will be a good opportunity for me to meet them as well."

"You want me to go with you, CB?"

"You heeled?"

"No."

"Well, you best not. But if I get to needing help, I'll scream out like a virgin on her wedding bed."

* * * *

The man Thurman described stood closest to the door. Two cowboys lined up beside him at the bar. The bartender was where bartenders should be. Wooly strode right up to the bar and next to the man wearing more guns than any one man should. He laid his axe handle on the bar top and nodded a greeting.

"Howdy, boys. I'm Marshal CB Wooly."

The man looked down at the club, and then looked up at Wooly with a grin. "Looks like you lost your axe blade, Marshal." Then the man laughed like he'd said something truly funny.

Wooly chuckled in turn. "Yup, left it stuck up some ol' boy's ass, I reckon."

The gunman laughed long and hard before saying, "We was just discussing you, Marshal Wooly. These boys were telling me you are looking for a deputy. I stand before you offering my talents."

"You're the lawman type, are you?" Wooly grinned.

"I'm damned accomplished with these here Remingtons," the man laughed.

Wooly didn't doubt it, and a plan popped into his mind. He looked back beyond the three men and then nodded in that direction. "I guess that woman's with you?"

As he'd hoped, all three heads jerked in that direction and Wooly used the distraction to pull his gun. When the man in the buckskins immediately turned back after finding no woman, Wooly planted his forty-five Colt Peacemaker in the space between the man's eyes and the upturned brim of his hat. With the barrel against skin, he thumbed back the hammer.

"Mister, I don't have to be standing in an outhouse to recognize the odor of shit."

The man with the gun pressed to his brains did not dare flinch, but he did laugh. "My new friends told me all about you,

Wooly," he carefully raised his eyes to stare up at the barrel of the Colt. "Is this the gun you used to shoot down Clay Bardoe?"

"Nope. I threw that gun in the Cimarron River outside Stillwater within a day's time of shooting ol' Clay. This here gun has yet to kill a man, but it's itching to."

Wooly then directed his words over this man's shoulder to the two cowboys. "You boys just stand steady."

"We're steady, Marshal," the closest man said.

"Damned steady," the furthest away emphasized with a tremor in his voice.

"Well, where do we go from here, Wooly?" the buckskinned man snickered.

If the man held an ounce of fear in him, Wooly could not detect it, and his guts tensed as a result thereof. "You are going to remove those Remingtons one at a time, and very slowly, you're going to eject the bullets here on the bar."

The man might not have known fear, but he proved to be no fool either. He slowly removed the gun from his left holster and started the process of unloading. He made it half way through the process when he looked over Wooly's shoulder and let go another laugh.

"I can't tell for sure which one he's got in his sights, Wooly," the man continued to laugh, "but there's a man behind you with a rifle pointed at either me or you."

Wooly pressed his gun even harder into the man's head and then let his eyes dart to the cowboy on the other side of the laughing man. The cowboy started to emphatically nod his head to confirm the fact.

Wooly took in a deep breath and turned his head just slightly to the right. "Are you friend or foe?" he hollered over his shoulder.

"I'm damned sure your friend, CB Wooly!" Came the answer. "But that rascal you got pinned is Laughing Billy Bemo. He's a murderous son of a bitch. Watch him closely."

Wooly recognized the voice he had not the pleasure to hear since the day he killed Clay Bardoe, and he smiled broadly at hearing it now. He then looked again to the men behind the laughing man. "You two cowboys hit the trail. And hit it now."

They didn't have to be told twice. It surprised Wooly that the bow-legged one could move so fast.

Once they were gone, the voice called out again from behind Wooly. "I'm coming around to your right side, CB."

"Come on, old friend."

When the short and very stout man stepped into his peripheral vision, Wooly smiled and said, "I don't know what you have been doing with yourself the last year or so, Floyd Danner, but I'm sure glad to see you now."

Many years before, Wooly put Danner in prison for a botched robbery of a stagecoach. The time in prison convinced Danner that the outlaw kind of life didn't much fit him. The two men didn't meet up again until Danner stood beside Wooly the day he went up against Bardoe. Danner did Wooly one hell of a service by keeping the curious and rambunctious mob at bay. The man showed grit and earned a special place in Wooly's heart.

"I've been doing just what I told you I was going to do," Danner replied. "I turned to doing the work of a lawman. I've served as a deputy both in Tombstone and Abilene. I've recently been working for Sheriff Joel Burbank down in Fort Worth. That's why I know of this bloodthirsty bastard."

Laughing Billy snorted and then giggled, "What is this? Some kind of family reunion?"

"Close your lips," Wooly barked, "and get to unloading them revolvers."

Danner had his Henry repeating rifle trained on Bemo's face. "I read you are looking to hire deputies. If you still got a position open, I'd like to apply," Danner said.

"Welcome aboard, Deputy Danner," Wooly grinned.

"I'm so moved by all this good will," Bemo said, "that for the first time in my life, I might just cry!" But then he laughed.

"If you'd allow me, Marshal," Danner growled, "I'll blow this bastard's face all over that back wall. We can do it now, or we will have to do it later."

The proposed words of violence set barkeeper Don Stroud to high-stepping to the far end of the bar in order to avoid the inevitable splattering of brains and blood.

"He ain't wanted here in Beaver City," Wooly answered with a disappointed sigh. "And as of yet, he ain't done anything that would justify us removing his face. I'll probably live to regret this decision, but once he has these guns emptied, I'd appreciate it, Floyd, if you'd just escort him to the city limits and see him on his way. Of course, if he gives you the slightest justifiable reason to do so between here and there, shoot him dead and leave him to rot."

Stroud and Bemo together, but for different reasons, offered up visible signs of relief.

* * * *

Ben Tackett did not particularly care for the man he'd agreed to do business with. As a matter of fact, Tackett found him downright despicable. Of course, if he held out until he found a hired killer he liked, Tackett would never finish the business of avenging Chuck Lawson's death. Tackett found this man's continual laughter most annoying, but his laugh seemed clearly as big a part of the man as the four guns strapped to his body.

Zed Martin and Shannon Wheeler gave Tackett ample notice the assassin might be riding in, but he showed up much sooner than Tackett anticipated. It was nearly sundown and just hours after Laughing Billy Bemo had been ridden out of Beaver City at the killing end of a Henry rifle. That last little bit of information came directly from Bemo, but earlier Zed Martin did a fine and entertaining job of retelling all that transpired in the Lone Star Saloon both before and after the new marshal made his entry. It sounded as if CB Wooly could be the kind of man Tackett would offer a swig of whiskey, and Tackett was particular who he drank with. He'd be damned if he'd ever drink with the likes standing before him now.

"Just so you got it clear," Tackett now said to Bemo, "I'm hiring you to kill only Buzz Libby and Dan Strapp. If you have to kill others to get to those two, that's on you, and I bare no responsibility. I'll pay you when you say the job is done."

"Why, hell fire, Mr. Tackett," Billy laughed, "how you know I ain't the type to just ride out a few days then ride back and say the deed is done when the deed ain't been done at all?"

Tackett didn't at all struggle for an answer. "I've lived a long time. I've seen all types. You ain't the kind of man, Laughing Billy, who would pass up any opportunity to kill."

"Well, you damned sure got me pegged on that one, Mr. Tackett," Billy guffawed. "Since I'm working for you, I want you to know this. I damned sure won't be passing up no opportunity to kill that CB Wooly and his new deputy, Floyd Danner. I don't forget or forgive being treated in such a manner. Now, if you got a problem with me doing that, it ain't going to stop me from killing them two, but I'd understand if you'd rather find you another man to run down Libby and Strapp."

Again, Tackett did not have to ponder a response. "CB Wooly is in the business of dealing with men like you. What goes on between you and him and his deputy is not on my conscience. But I will say this, Laughing Billy, I hope you run across Libby and Strapp before you do Wooly, because I ain't sure you got the metal to take on that old bull."

The hired killer threw back his head and laughed enthusiastically, but Tackett got the distinct impression he really didn't find what Tackett said to be all that funny.

* * * *

"Not a single shot was fired! Not one! No blood, my darling! Not even a drop!"

Margaret Smith took a deep breath and held her tongue. The bold manner in which CB Wooly dispensed of a seemingly very bad man quickly became the talk of the town, and now that talk found its way to her marriage bed as well. Margaret wished for something close by and heavy she could use to apply to her husband's head to help him sleep. If he did not pipe down soon, she would surely crawl from the bed in search of just such an object.

"I do not find pleasure, Margaret, in pointing out that you have so far been wrong about our new marshal," Elijah clucked. He then chuckled, "Blood City! Indeed!"

Maybe she had misspoken, yet she'd be damned before admitting as much to Elijah, but she found herself desiring to confess it to the new marshal himself. Literally a dozen or more episodes of self-rebuking had not forced from Margaret's mind the temptation of paying CB Wooly a visit. Nothing she intended was lascivious, but her motives were still less than proper. She'd found pleasure in the way the man looked at her once, and she could stand to have him look at her that way a second time. She also could not deny she found Wooly both in appearance and actions to be most intriguing.

"You must admit, Margaret, it took great courage to walk right up to an outlaw like that Laughing Billy. By God, CB Wooly is one hell of a man!"

Margaret rolled over in bed to face the direction in which her husband wasn't. It disturbed her more than just a little that the man she married seemed even more infatuated than her with the town's new marshal.

* * * *

Laughing Billy Bemo declined the offer to spend the night in the bunkhouse with the cowboys. He left the Tackett ranch just before sunset with good directions on how to find the Four-Deuces ranch. Bemo intended to put the night to good use. In the dark, he could scout without being seen and by morning would have working knowledge of the layout of the ranch and the lands surrounding it. Before the sun came up, he'd have a plan in mind, and with any luck at all, he'd have it put in place before the great ball of fire could mark mid-day on a sundial.

Bemo beamed with excitement about the prospect of quickly putting an end to the two cowboys. A great deal of money would be his the moment he accomplished the deed. More importantly, the sooner the cowboys died, the quicker Bemo could turn his sights on Wooly and Danner.

Bemo took pride in living a life immune to ridicule. He'd never been bullied or cowed, and until today, he'd never known humiliation. Wooly did what no man had ever been able to do before. He'd rendered Laughing Billy Bemo helpless. He'd been run out of town like a rat out of a chicken coop. Townspeople had looked on while Bemo fought the urge to bow his head. Bemo never before bowed his head, and he damned sure didn't start doing it today. Instead of bowing, he'd laughed.

"Why you laugh so much, you silly son of a bitch?" Danner had called out from behind him on their trek out of town. Bemo turned in his saddle to look back on the deputy riding a brightly colored pinto. The powerful Henry rifle lay menacingly across the gullet of his saddle. That spoke of the confidence the deputy had in his abilities. Most who knew Bemo's reputation, as most assuredly did Danner, would have the rifle up, ready, and pointed at the back side of Bemo's black heart.

"The world is an evil place where a lot of awful things happen, and that makes me giddy," Bemo emphasized his point with thunderous laughter.

"Well, it's a damned annoying habit you've fallen into. I wish the hell you'd just swallow your tongue and choke to death on it," Danner said.

Bemo snickered a little before responding, "I wish you'd let me load just one of my pistols. We could back off about fifty yards from each other and have at it. You got fifteen rounds in that Henry. I'd only have six in my pistol, but I bet I'd take you out of the saddle before you could me."

This time Danner did the laughing. "That ain't my way of gun fighting. With a gun, I'd either kill you really up close and by surprise, or I'd shoot you from a distance with my rifle that those Remingtons couldn't match in range."

Just when Bemo thought Danner said all he had to say, he started back up. "Tell you a deal I will make you, though. We can jump off these horses, toss our guns aside, and go at it hand and foot. I'd beat you to the ground like a stepchild and stomp on you like a cockroach!"

Bemo laughed, but he did not take Danner's offer to engage in fisticuffs. Danner stood a head shorter than Bemo, but looked as solid as a blacksmith's anvil.

The two men didn't exchange another word until they reached the edge of town.

"I'm stopping here," Danner said. "You keep on riding. I promise you this. If you start loading those Remingtons at a distance I can see you doing it, that will also be a distance I can put a bullet through your heart, and I'd love the opportunity to do just that."

Bemo didn't immediately respond. He rode out about twenty paces before slowly turning his horse to face Danner.

"And I promise you this, deputy. Today, you and your boss became dead men. You are still walking and still talking, but you are as good as already burning in hell."

Bemo said all of that and never even cracked a smile. He would bet the significance therein was not lost on Floyd Danner.

CHAPTER SEVEN

One Sorry Bastard

Hound Olivo and Rob Cotton rode out from the Four-Twos headquarters an hour past sunup. The foreman, John George, dispatched them to the far north pastures to wrangle back some wild ponies for breaking. Olivo remained as quiet as usual. He just had no more to say this morning than he did any other morning. Besides, Olivo preferred listening over talking, and that proved a good thing for anyone teamed up with Rob Cotton. It had been said, and Olivo believed it, that the first thing to go to sleep every night on Cotton was his lips, because those were what he worked hardest throughout the day. Olivo and Cotton had been in the saddle for about fifteen minutes and for fifteen minutes, Cotton had been orating over the hottest topic to hit No-Man's-Land since the region had been denied territorial status.

"Yup, I most certainly have been gnawing on the idea. As a matter of fact, I've thought a couple of times over the years I might take right to being a lawman. But I'll just sit back for a while and see who else comes forward. If CB Wooly don't have the deputies he wants in the next month or so, I might throw my hat in the ring. Hell, the work has to be a lot easier than wrangling wild horses."

Olivo nodded every few minutes if he agreed and shook his head when he didn't. He did say "Uh-hu" a couple of times and "Nope" once, but that had been his only contributions to the discussion, which didn't bother Cotton in the least bit. Cotton yapped on about what it took to make a good deputy, as if he really had any idea, when Olivo caught sight of a rider approaching from their flank at a gallop.

"Rob," he interrupted. "We got a rider coming on hard. Olivo pulled his rifle from the scabbard and felt relieved when Cotton hushed up and did the same.

"You recognize him?" Cotton asked.

"Nope. But looks like he's wearing buckskins."

The region had been cleared of raiding Comanche warriors for some years now, and both Olivo and Cotton had helped in that clearing. Just the sight of buckskins still served to make Olivo jittery. He considered the possibility that the approaching rider could be a renegade who had escaped from the reservation situated a good long ways southeast of No-Man's-Land. Then Olivo saw the golden hair flying in the wake of the fast riding horse.

"Ain't no Indian," he shouted to Cotton, "and he ain't got no guns in his hands either."

"What the hell's he intending, Hound? Maybe he's aiming to ride right over us?"

"I don't know," Olivo said, as he raised his rifle and took aim, "but I intend to be ready for just about anything. I suggest you do the same, Rob."

Rob followed both Olivo's lead and suggestion.

Within seconds both men were hollering warnings for the rider to halt. Olivo just started to think he wasn't going to stop when all of a sudden, he did. If the man would have traveled just another ten feet, Olivo would have pulled his trigger. As it was, the man positioned himself right between Olivo and Cotton. Either one of them could have reached out and touched him with their rifle barrels, and the damnedest thing was the man just laughed his ass off.

"Hell, boys," the man said through his laughter, "in this country you shoot men for riding hard and laughing?"

Olivo thought about the question, let out a long-held breath, and then slid his rifle back in the scabbard. Even though the man wore four pistols, he damned sure seemed a jolly type, and Olivo didn't have the heart to shoot the jolly type.

* * * *

Laughing Billy just sat and chuckled until the other cowboy decided he had not committed a shooting offense and put his rifle away as well.

"Mister," this cowboy asked, "are you drunk or just crazy?"

Bemo laughed hard at that one before pulling two of the Remingtons faster than a wink. He couldn't help but laugh harder at the surprise in the cowboys' eyes on how quickly they came to find themselves on the other end of pointed barrels.

"I am not presently drunk, boys, but I'm always crazy. I could not help but see the surprise on your faces on how quick I am with my pistols. Take me at my word, I'm as accurate as I am quick, and I can't miss at this distance."

"What's this all about?" the same cowboy spoke again. The other seemed to be a man of few words. Both, however, looked to be men of common sense who knew they now held anything but the upper hand.

"Would either of you gents be named Libby or Strapp?"

"Neither of us is Libby or Strapp," the spokesman announced. "I'm Rob Cotton and this here is Hound Olivo. It ain't that he's unfriendly, but ol' Hound don't have much to say."

Bemo found that funny. After he laughed he said, "Well, in that case, you two will have to do. First thing I need is for you both to pull out those sidearms and toss them to the ground."

The one called Hound hesitated at first, but they both eventually complied.

"Now, crawl off those horses," Bemo grinned. "And stand clear of them guns."

When both cowboys were on the ground, Bemo holstered the revolver in his right hand and kept the other trained on the men as he first removed one rifle from a standing horse and gave it fling and then pulled the other and did the same thing.

"Get your hands high in the air, fellers," he ordered.

Bemo nodded at Cotton. "You'll be staying with me."

He then turned his gaze on Olivo. "They call me Laughing Billy Bemo and I'm a happy and killing son of a bitch. So, you best listen close to what I have to say. You are going to ride back to the ranch and deliver this message. There's a good-sized hill one mile east of here. From on top, a man has a clear view in all directions. I'm going to take Mr. Cotton and ride back to that hill. If Strapp and Libby don't come out to meet me on that hilltop before sunset, I'll be killing Mr. Cotton. Anyone riding with Strapp and Libby can expect the same. Now, tell me, Mr. Olivo, which one of those hands in the air is your gun hand?"

Hound Olivo once again hesitated, but he finally flexed the fingers of his right hand. In the next blink of an eye, Bemo put a bullet clean through that hand.

The cowboys' horses bolted as Olivo let out a scream and grabbed his damaged hand with the one not bleeding.

Bemo howled in laugher and announced. "Catch them horses, boys, and don't forget that if I can put a bullet through a hand, I can just as easily put one through a heart, or two hearts if need be."

* * * *

Hound Olivo stood before Stew Graybow with his good hand gripping his bad and delivered the message the laughing man dictated. He experienced a great deal of pain, but felt more concerned about his boss's reaction than he did the hole through his hand.

Graybow let out a stream of profanity and kicked violently at the dirt around his feet with one boot and then the other. "That cussed Ben Tackett has hired him a ruthless killer," he bellowed.

Foreman John George was the only other man privy to the discussion in front of Mr. Graybow's ranch house. "You want me to gather the boys and ride out to kill the bastard?"

Graybow let out more curses, but it seemed obvious to Olivo that the old man carefully contemplated his options. Several tense moments passed before he growled, "No. Go get Strapp and Libby and send them this way."

George hurried away to do as told, and Olivo stood by, holding his tongue as usual, and wondering what Graybow held in store for him.

"Hound," Graybow finally grumbled, "you ain't no use to me as a cow hand in your present condition. So, I'm going to send you on a vital journey."

Olivo breathed a sigh of relief. He'd feared Graybow, an awfully hard man, would have held him responsible for Rob Cotton being used as ransom.

"You get that hand doctored, then I want you to ride out for Santa Fe in the New Mexico Territory. I want you to ride hard and I want you to ride fast. There's a man there known by many. He's an Apache Indian. His Christian name is John Paul. You find him, and tell him I'll pay the price he asks to travel here and do some killing. Ben Tackett has started a war, and I intend to win it."

* * * *

Dan Strapp could tell by the look in the foreman's eyes and the tone of his voice, but he asked anyway, "Ain't gonna to be pleasant, is it?"

John George twisted his face into a grimace and then sighed, "Hell, Dan, is seeing old man Graybow ever pleasant?"

George had smoothly dodged the question which allowed Buzz Libby to almost make a fairly good point.

"We're shoveling shit out of stalls, Dan. How much worse can it get for a couple of genuine ol' cowboys?"

If Libby held any further words from the sunny-side, he didn't share them during the walk from the barn to the ranch house. Strapp remained silent as well. Graybow sat in a rocker up on his grand front porch. He motioned Strapp and Libby up and pointed at two other chairs he'd pulled close.

"Take a load off, boys," Graybow said in his typically gruff manner.

Strapp's ass barely touched the seat before Graybow started right in with what he had to say.

"Ben Tackett has hired a gun hand. Today, he jumped Cotton and Olivo. He shot Olivo through the hand and kept Cotton as a bargaining chip. He's holding Cotton on what I believe to be

Walter's Hill. If you two men don't ride out to meet him, he's going to kill Cotton.

"Now, I've considered my options. I could take our men and ride on that hill, and Cotton would die for sure. Because this man kills for a living, I'm willing to bet he's real handy with his firearms. That being the case, he'd get at least two of us and maybe more. But if you two rode up there alone, I'd be assured of losing only three men versus four or God knows how many.

"Of course, I can't order you two to ride up there and get yourselves killed. But I can't have you staying here. The way I see it, you have two options. You can ride up and see what you can do to save ol' Cotton, or you can ride out of here in some other direction and save yourselves. If that's what you choose to do, I'd think no less of you. You're not gunmen, and I expect you have little to no chance of making a successful stand against someone who is. That's all I got to say."

Libby summed up his position in one word. "Damn."

Strapp felt a need to say a few words more. "Mr. Graybow, if it was you that was riding against this man, how would you do it?"

Graybow scratched at his white beard for several long seconds before offering an answer. "If I was you boys, I don't know that I wouldn't ride in some other direction. But if I was to make a run at Walter's Hill, I'd do so with my favorite gun in hand and blazing away as if there was no tomorrow because chances are good there ain't going to be."

Strapp stood and held his right hand out to the older man. "You've been a fair enough boss, Mr. Graybow. So long."

* * * *

Dan Strapp strode straight out to the barn and immediately started to saddle his horse. Buzz Libby worked at doing the same.

"Where you headed, Dan?" Libby asked.

"In my way of thinking, there's only one place I can go. I'm headed to Walter's Hill."

"You'll most surely die, Dan."

"If I do, I brought it on myself. I got to do what I can to see to it that Rob Cotton don't die for my sins."

"Ain't you going to say that this is all my fault?" Libby asked.

"Nope. If that needs to be said, I guess you'll be the one to say it."

Strapp got his horse bridled only heartbeats ahead of Buzz Libby. He swung into the saddle and looked down on what had been, in all things considered, a decent friend.

"Hope I'll be seeing you around, Buzz Libby."

"You'll be seeing me around, you son of a bitch," Libby said as he put the finishing touches on readying his mount, "because I'm going with you."

* * * *

Laughing Billy looked down at the man lying on his belly with his arms behind his back and his wrists strapped to his ankles, and couldn't help but asking, "Do you ever stop talking?"

Rob Cotton strained his neck to look up. "I talk a blue streak in normal situations, but I talk even more when I'm nervous."

Bemo had to force a laugh. "I wish the hell you'd shut up. You done wore out my left ear and my right one is starting to tingle."

The man talked about anything and everything and just simply nothing at all. Bemo considered a couple of times of just putting a bullet in him for a little peace and quiet, but that didn't work into his plan.

"You ever been up in the Rocky Mountains?" Cotton asked.

"What the hell would make you think about mountains?" Bemo chuckled rather blandly.

"All kind of things are going through my mind," Cotton replied.

"Yeah, and right out your mouth," Bemo added. "Hell, man, I'm known for my laughing, but you make me want to scream."

"I went up in the Rockies back in about seventy," Cotton started.

Laughing Billy grabbed up a rock about the size of a small apple and forced it into the open mouth. In a matter of seconds Cotton began to gag. Then he started to flop on his belly like a fish out of water. Being hog-tied, it was all he could do, but at least he flopped instead of talking. For the first time in at least two hours, Bemo had himself a true laughing fit. He enjoyed watching Cotton suffer and had fell deep into wondering just how long he could go without passing out when he noticed two riders pop into view over the horizon. They rode from the direction of the Four-Twos ranch. Bemo reached down and jerked the rock from Rob Cotton's mouth.

"Looks like we got company coming," he giggled. He then busied himself searching in all directions for any signs of other riders and a trap. In a matter of moments, he felt certain the two were all who were coming and he turned his attention wholly on them and their approach.

Soon they drew close enough for Bemo to determine they had pulled their rifles and were carrying them barrels up with one hand wrapped around the cocking lever and trigger guard on the small of the stock. They clearly rode in no hurry to get to the top of the hill since they kept their horses at a walk. When Bemo knew for sure they were close enough to see him, he stepped about ten feet away from Cotton and pulled the Remingtons from the right and left holsters. He held the gun in his left hand down alongside his leg. He raised the right at a forty-five-degree angle to the ground so the riders could plainly see the gun aimed at Rob Cotton, who continued to gasp for air, but rested from his flopping fit.

Bemo knew they understood his gesture when they reined their horses to a stop about seventy-five yards out. It looked to him as if they exchanged a few words before starting again in his direction, this time even more cautiously than before.

* * * *

Dan Strapp did as Buzz Libby suggested and pulled back the hammer on a round already chambered in his Winchester. They both agreed not yet to point their rifles. The man in buckskins had a gun clearly pointed at Rob Cotton's head. They both feared that if they brought the rifles up to the ready, the man would shoot Cotton out right.

"The son of a bitch has him trussed up like a pig ready for slaughter," Libby mumbled under his breath as they moved slowly up the hill.

They were about fifty yards from the gunman and Cotton when the man with a gun in each hand hollered out to them.

"That's close enough, fellers. I don't care if you keep those revolvers on your hips, but put those rifles away and get down off them horses."

Libby quickly came up with a response he shared with only Strapp. "That ain't no good. Let's charge him from here and fire for all we're worth."

"We do that," Strapp responded, "and he will kill Cotton for sure."

"If we don't, he'll kill us for sure," Libby hissed.

"We came to keep him from killing Cotton," Strapp insisted. "If we charge him and he kills Cotton and gets one or both of us, what have we managed to do?"

This time Libby offered no quick response. Finally, he exhaled, "Hell if I know."

"Let's do what he says," Strapp pleaded. "We'll still have our sidearms."

"You any good with a pistol?" Libby asked.

"You know I ain't," Strapp answered.

"Well, I know you are now a damned sight better than me. My right arm ain't yet got back to regular since that dog got at it.

I'll be shooting with my left hand and I might as well be shooting with either one of my durn feet!"

Several long seconds passed before Libby sighed hard and then slid his rifle back into its scabbard. Strapp took a deep breath and then slid his in also. Both cowboys swung out of their saddles at the same time.

They started side by side toward the two men on the hill. Both had their hands resting on the grips of their still holstered revolvers. Libby reached across his body with his left hand to do so.

"No matter what happens," Strapp felt obliged to say, "you're a hell of a man, Buzz Libby, for coming this far."

The response took so long in coming that Strapp had practically given up on one.

"I'm a damned fool, Dan Strapp, and so are you for sticking by my side all these years."

* * * *

Billy Bemo let the two men advance to about thirty paces, then he let out with a squeal of laughter stopping the two cowboys in their tracks. At that moment he cocked both the gun pointed to the ground and the one pointed at Rob Cotton's now quivering head.

"I'm hoping you boys are Strapp and Libby," Bemo said in a tone dancing with merriment.

His joy apparently left the two men momentarily without words and with looks in their eyes as uneasy as a herd of wild horses in a thunder storm. Finally, though, the one to Bemo's right spoke in a voice that sounded anything but confident.

"I'm Buzz Libby and this is Dan Strapp and you got to be one sorry bastard."

Bemo could not help but laugh long and hard at Libby's bravado.

When he finished, he kept a grin on his face and said, "I didn't honestly think you boys would show."

Strapp, this time, did the talking. "We ain't the kind to let an innocent man die in our stead."

"Well, I do declare that is down-right dandy," Bemo winked and grinned, "but awfully stupid." He promptly pulled a trigger resulting in the messy destruction of Rob Cotton's head.

Bemo learned a long time before that seconds counted as hours in a gun battle, and that shock and surprise could buy precious seconds. This fight produced no exceptions to that rule. Both Strapp and Libby were momentarily stunned by the shot that took Cotton's life, and a moment was all Bemo needed. He turned the gun in his right hand at Libby and quickly discharged the remaining five bullets while simultaneously turning the left one on Strapp to empty the six rounds it still held. When those two guns were emptied he dropped them and pulled the two remaining Remingtons from his gun belt, but they were not needed. Both Strapp and Libby had fallen. Libby lay on his left side and did nothing but bleed. Strapp lay on his back with his head turned to the right and his eyes open and blinking as his mouth formed words Bemo could not hear.

Libby's body fell closest to Bemo. As he strode by to get closer to Strapp, he put a bullet through Libby's head just for good measure. Strapp jerked hard at the sound of the single shot and his mouth seemed to start moving faster.

Bemo nudged Strapp with the toe of his boot as he looked down with a wide grin. "Who you talking to, feller?"

Strapp's words came haltingly and barely above a whisper. "My ma. See her over there? Came to take me to heaven. Told me not to be skeer'd."

Bemo pointed in the direction of the dying man's gaze. "Is she over there?"

"You do see her. Don't you?"

"Nope," Bemo said before nearly busting a gut. "All I see is the ol' devil and he's coming to get you, cowboy!"

Dan Strapp let out with a fearful moan, and Bemo laughed all that harder. It looked to him as if tears were starting to form in Strapp's eyes, and Bemo stopped laughing. A crying man was not funny. A crying man was despicable. He quickly raised his right boot and planted the sole of it against Strapp's throat and pushed down hard and kept pushing until the eyes stopped blinking and stared blankly and the mouth stopped moving and only gaped.

Bemo untied Rob Cotton's horse and picked up Strapp and Libby's hats. He used the hats to slap at the three cow ponies to send them running in the general direction of the Four-Twos. He stuffed the hats in his saddle bag and considered cutting the rope binding Cotton's wrists and ankles, but didn't. Cotton needed to be found by the hands of Four-Twos ranch just like he died.

CHAPTER EIGHT

Simple Act of Kindness

Zed Martin stood alongside Ben Tackett and watched Ward Avants trying to ride the buck out of a green pony when Laughing Billy Bemo rode up to the corral. Bemo laughed a greeting and Mr. Tackett solemnly nodded one back in return. Bemo, still in the saddle, busied himself with removing two hats from his saddle bags. He dropped the hats on the ground at Mr. Tackett's feet.

"Those belong to Buzz Libby and Dan Strapp, both of which are now dead men," Bemo said in his laughing manner that tended to make Martin nervous.

"To get those two, I had to kill another man by the name of Cotton," Bemo continued, "In a way, in which I'm sure you would not approve, but it didn't cost you a cent."

Martin looked on as Mr. Tackett studied the two hats at his feet before responding to Bemo. "I'll give you this, Laughing Billy, you do work fast," Tackett said with no apparent joy.

Martin endured more of Bemo's laughter before the man in buckskins responded. "Well, Mr. Tackett, if you was to hire me to paint your house, I might agree to do so, but I'd probably never get the job done. But, when you hire me to kill, you're hiring me to do something I'm both good at and do, God help me, *so* enjoy."

Martin could tell by the look on his boss's face that those words had not set right with him, and evidently, so had Bemo. That's when the hired killer added, "I sense, Mr. Tackett, you don't approve of my type. Yet, it's clear to me I was able to scratch an itch you couldn't reach."

Ben Tackett seemed to think hard on Bemo's words. The old man nodded his head a couple of times before responding, "I reckon I'm hypocritical in that way, Laughing Billy. I also find what whores do to make a living kind of despicable, but I've paid them to scratch a few itches as well."

Martin laughed right along with Bemo this time. Before Bemo even stopped laughing, he said to Mr. Tackett, "I'll draw my pay now, Boss Tackett. There's a recently widowed lady just as pretty as a flower two day's ride south of here. I'm going to go spend a little time with her, and then I'll be back to kill Wooly and his deputy." He then went on to give explicit directions to the widow's abode just in case Tackett needed him before he decided to come back on his own.

Martin stayed in place beside Bemo and his horse as Tackett walked off to the house to get the man's pay. Martin's curiosity got the best of him long before Tackett reached his front door. "How did you kill ol' Rob Cotton, Laughing Billy?"

"I trussed him up like a pig, and blew the top of his head off. I left him all tied up as a warning to the rest of that outfit as to the kind of man they're dealing with."

As if just funny as hell, Bemo then went on to explain to Martin how he'd run upon Cotton and Olivo and how he'd shot Olivo through the hand and used Cotton as bait to draw in Libby and Strapp. Martin felt Strapp and Libby got what they had coming to them, but he'd be damned if he thought any of it the least bit funny. He found himself suddenly very relieved this man would soon ride away from the Tackett ranch.

After Mr. Tackett returned with the money and Laughing Billy got on his way, Martin turned to his boss. "I don't mind sayin', Mr. Tackett, that I hope that's the last we'll see of that man."

"I hope for the same, young Zed, but the fact is that will rest solely on the actions of Stew Graybow."

Zed Martin found no comfort in that at all.

* * * *

CB Wooly strolled down the main street of his new town, just out and about and being seen, when he looked up and saw a familiar figure approaching on horseback. You didn't ride with a man as long as Wooly did this one not to immediately recognize the way he sat a saddle.

"Well, I'll be damned," Wooly mumbled under his breath to no one but himself. He then raised a hand and waived as a smile spread across his face. The horse and rider were still well outside conversing distance when Wooly hollered out, "Damn good to see you, Walt Tabor! What brings you to Beaver City?"

Tabor waited until he rode close enough to rein his horse to a halt and swing out of the saddle. "Good to see you was well, CB Wooly. I'm hoping you are still in need of deputies."

Wooly and Tabor had served together as United States deputy marshals prior and up to the time Clay Bardoe started his murderous rampage. Tabor proved himself to be a capable and dependable lawman up to that time. Next to Clay Bardoe, Tabor had been the best partner Wooly had ever ridden with. Now, Wooly could not help but recall what ended Tabor's service as a lawman.

Wooly was away and burying his loving old mother back in Virginia when Tabor found himself face to face with Clay Bardoe and forced to act. It came down to both men drawing their weapons, and Tabor ended up throwing his aside in order to save his life. Moments later, he removed his badge and tossed it down as well. Wooly never faulted the man for doing so. Without a doubt, if he had not backed down, he would not have lived to ride into Beaver City on this day nearly two years later.

At this moment, there on the main street, it greatly surprised Wooly that Tabor had come seeking a job. The last time Wooly laid eyes on Tabor, he wore the clothing of a common townsman like a store clerk or even a bank teller. He had surely cast aside all aspects and manners of a lawman. Now, he made his appearance adorned as one who had just stepped from the pages of a western dime novel. From where he stood, Wooly could see two revolvers stuck in the new-fangled Mexican loop holsters designed for quick drawing. On top of his head was a fancy kind of hat old Buffalo Bill Cody might wear in one of his Wild West shows.

"You look a tad bit different from the time we last spoke," Wooly said as he reached out and enthusiastically shook the hand extended his way.

"I'm a different man than I was then, CB," Tabor said with conviction.

"How so, Walt?" Wooly couldn't help but ask.

Tabor reached into a vest pocket, pulled out a silver dollar and flipped it to Wooly. "Toss that coin up in the air as far as you can toss it."

Although a most unusual request, Wooly didn't pause to give it any thought. He just gave the coin a fling. He no sooner let it go than Tabor pulled one of his revolvers just as smooth as a lady's butt, and slick as a whistle, to immediately blow a hole right through the middle of the flying silver dollar.

"Damn, Walt! That's some kind of fancy shooting," Wooly had to admit.

"I tried my hand at numerous occupations, CB, but settled on farming. I couldn't make a go of it. I ended up spending all my money on bullets. I toiled hour after hour on my little piece of land shooting at cans and bottles until I finally reached a point of being damned good at shooting at anything I aimed a gun at. At the distance that separated me and Clay Bardoe back then, I can now put a bullet through a man's eye. I'm that good, CB."

"Well, you just proved that, but hell, Walt, you don't have to justify to me," Wooly started before being cut off.

"I do, CB. You see, in those books that have been written, you are depicted as a hero, and justly so. Me? I'm depicted as a coward, and justly so. Yet, that's a title that I'm driven to prove false."

"You don't have to prove a damned thing to me, Walt Tabor," Wooly said forcibly.

"I appreciate that, CB. But I have to prove it to myself, and I have to prove it to the world. I'm hoping to do that here in Beaver City as one of CB Wooly's deputies."

"Walt, I'd hire you as a deputy even if you hadn't gone and become a fancy dressed shootist," Wooly ribbed.

Tabor grinned wide and stuck out his hand to seal the deal. "I won't let you down, CB."

"You never did before," Wooly said as he again shook his old friend's hand.

* * * *

"Floyd Danner, I want you to meet Walt Tabor. Walt, this here is Floyd Danner. Floyd, Walt's joining up with us."

Nearly three hours passed since Wooly spoke those words. Now he'd retired to his room for the evening, was well into his whiskey, and looking up at Floyd Danner who just dropped in to say his piece.

Earlier, when the introductions were made inside the yet to be completed marshal's office, Wooly studied each of his deputies' eyes for a reaction to the arrangement. He expected Tabor to recognize the name of the man who faithfully watched his back the day he killed Clay Bardoe. Wooly knew for a fact Danner would recognize the name Walt Tabor. Back in the Oklahoma Territory, the name had grown synonymous with the color yellow.

Tabor did indeed express knowledge of Floyd Danner, and the newest deputy enthusiastically extended his hand in friendship. Wooly could tell by the look in Danner's eyes he, too, knew the name Walt Tabor. Although he acted gracious enough not to make mention of that fact, Danner hesitated before gripping Tabor's hand. Wooly observed that Tabor noticed the hesitancy, but he took it in stride like a man accustomed to being shunned in far more blatant ways than this.

Now, Wooly remained seated, looking up at Danner. He would have preferred getting up and offering his deputy a seat, but the room bore only one chair and Wooly did not prefer Danner witnessing the difficulty he'd have getting out of that chair because of already too much whiskey consumed at such an early hour of the evening.

"What's on your mind, Floyd?" Wooly asked as if he didn't already know.

"It's Walt Tabor, CB. I'd be less than honest with you if I didn't confess I'm not wholly comfortable with having him at my side, and I'd be downright uncomfortable should it come to a time and place when I have to depend on him having my back."

"I understand your concern, Floyd," Wooly nodded sincerely, "because you only know what you might have read or what someone might have told you. There's a lot to the Tabor story you don't know. I rode a good long distance with the man, and I always found him dependable and trustworthy. I think it's a crying shame that, for all the courageous things I saw that man do, he's practically been ruined for being in a bad situation and making the only truly good choice there was to make. If he'd done a damned thing different that night in the whore house, he'd just simply been killed, and what good would that have done?"

Wooly sat in silence and studied Danner as he sucked on a tooth and thought hard about all Wooly had said.

"Okay, then, CB. If you got that much stock in the man, how could I have any less? And the point you make is a good one. There wasn't but one man that could stand against Clay Bardoe and walk away to talk about it. Ain't that the truth?" Danner concluded with a chuckle.

It was kind of the truth, and it kind of wasn't. Someday, CB decided there and then, he'd have to tell both Danner and Tabor the rest of that old story. But it wouldn't be tonight. Tonight, Wooly would just keep the truth to himself and try to extinguish the flames with yet more whiskey.

* * * *

Although her husband preferred her to go to bed when he did, Margaret stayed up late baking two pies, one rhubarb and the other a peach, and both were for the town's three newest citizens. Any news at all, normally spread like wildfire among the citizens of Beaver City. It turned out that any news dealing with CB Wooly spread like hellfire. The latest man to be hired as a deputy rode into town only a few hours before sunset. Before dark everyone knew his identity and that Wooly had pinned a deputy badge on him.

To Margaret's amusement her husband, Elijah, found two occasions on this day to be critical of the new town marshal. The same man over whom he previously expressed nothing short of idolatry. Very early in the day Elijah went out to sweep the front porch and to his delight looked up to see CB Wooly strolling south bound on the Smith's side of the main street and headed in their direction. But when he approached at nearly a half a block away from their store, Wooly crossed the street and continued to walk south.

"He seemed almost intent in not even looking in my direction. I got the distinct impression," Elijah practically whined, "that he intentionally avoided me. Why would he do such a thing, Margaret?"

Margaret knew the reason, but how could she tell Elijah? It certainly was not her husband Wooly wished to avoid. When the news came shortly after dark that Wooly had hired Walt Tabor, Elijah expressed astonishment over the marshal's decision to hire a notorious coward. Margaret could not help but think the hiring of Walt Tabor spoke of something both sympathetic and loyal in Wooly's character. For that reason, she stayed up late baking the pies.

She had contemplated a welcoming basket all day long, but time and time again came up with reasons why she should maintain the same safe distance Wooly made efforts to keep. She finally convinced herself that more existed of CB Wooly than what met the eye or filled the pages of a dime novel. With that in mind, she could not come up with a reason good enough to prevent her from performing a simple act of kindness. Besides, she wasn't making pies for just one man, but for three. Or at least, that was what Margaret wanted her conscience to believe.

CHAPTER NINE

Just Wooly's Coward

By nine the next morning Margaret had her basket of pies in hand and made her way to the newly erected wooden structure that served as Beaver City's marshal's office and jail. She walked nearly half way there when she suddenly felt through the soles of her shoes the pounding of many hooves on hard ground. In the next moment she heard them as well. Riders approaching the town hell bent for leather were never a good thing. Margaret pressed her back to the building she walked alongside of and waited for the thundering troop to pass. Other pedestrians also moved to places of safety. Some were mothers tugging at the arms of little ones.

All too soon, four horsemen galloped into sight at the edge of town, and they did not slow down once they reached the rows of buildings and houses marking the town proper. The lead rider could be identified by his long snow-white beard and hair. Stew Graybow and three of his cowboys galloped in an awful hurry to get wherever they were going.

Once they passed her by, Margaret stepped out into the street to watch their progression. She learned in the next few seconds that they shared her destination. Margaret Smith lifted the hem of her day dress an inch or so and now hurried toward the partially completed building that might one day play a part in deterring ruffians from riding pell-mell through town.

* * * *

Wooly sat alone in his office when he first heard the sound of fast approaching horses. Danner and Tabor were out making themselves known to the town folk. Wooly picked up his axe handle and walked outside to wait and see what'd be riding in on the backs of the incoming horses. By that time Danner came in a hurry from one direction and Tabor from the other.

Now with men he trusted on his left and right, he stood steady as the four horsemen brought their winded mounts to a halt. A man with a rugged face framed by long white whiskers glared down at Wooly with steely eyes.

"My name is Stew Graybow and these here are what's left of my ranch hands," the man thundered.

"Glad to meet you, Mr. Graybow. My name is," Wooly started before rudely being talked over by the loud speaking Graybow.

"I know your damned name, and this ain't no social call, Wooly."

Wooly took a moment to chuckle before saying calmly, "Well, then, what kind of call is it, Graybow?"

"Ben Tackett, a sorry bastard if there ever was one, has hired himself an assassin. I don't recall the man's name, but he laughs a whole hell of a lot and wears buckskins."

"That'd be Laughing Billy Bemo," Danner said under his breath.

Wooly nodded his agreement.

"Should have let me shoot his face off," Danner added.

Wooly nodded his agreement.

"The killing son of a bitch has done murdered three of my hands and shot a forth one and he did it on my ranch land," Graybow spewed.

"I hate hearing that, Graybow. I honestly do," Wooly said while shaking his head in disgust, "but I have no jurisdiction outside these town limits."

"Jurisdiction?" Graybow bellowed. "Do you think I'm here asking you to handle this matter? Hell, I ain't here asking a damned thing from you. I'll handle this my own way. You asked what kind of call this is? It's a warning call. I'm warning you that a range war has been started and I'm warning you and your deputies to stay out of my way."

Wooly theatrically arched his eyebrows and looked first at Danner and then at Tabor. "Boys, are we being threatened?"

Before either deputy could offer an answer, Graybow shouted one. "You damned better believe you are!"

Wooly stepped up closer to Graybow's horse. "Well, in that case, Graybow, I'm here and now decreeing a new law in Beaver City. From this day hence forth, you and your men are prohibited from carrying hand guns in my town. You can ride in with a rifle for protection from your ranch to this town, but once in town, said rifles will remain in the scabbards. Boys," Wooly said with another look to his left and right, "did that sound official enough?"

"Who the hell do you think you are?" Graybow growled.

"I know who the hell I am," Wooly said with a grin. "What's important is that you know who the hell I am."

"You think you scare me?" Graybow huffed.

Wooly stepped even closer. "I imagine it's been a long time since you've had your ass whipped, and you know why that is?"

"Why don't you tell me?" Graybow hissed.

"Because most men would find your ass too old to whip, but you ain't that much older than me. What? Maybe ten years or so? That ain't enough difference in years to keep me from pulling you off that horse and whipping your ass like your mama used to do it."

"You talk real tough with that club in your hands," Graybow said with a voice quivering with rage.

Wooly tossed his axe handle to the ground and removed his revolver and handed it over to Walt Tabor. "Now I ain't got nothing but my hands, teeth, and feet. Crawl your ass off that horse, you loud-mouthed bastard!"

Stew Graybow's face turned the color of overly ripe tomatoes and he let go with a string of profanities, but he did not crawl his ass off the horse.

Wooly quickly surveyed the faces of the other mounted men and found nothing there but fear. "Take your cow pokes and ride the hell out of my town."

"Wooly, you've said words here today you will live to regret," Graybow shouted. "You've made in me the worst enemy you've yet to face."

Wooly took his gun back from Tabor and held it at his side. "Ride out of here slow and easy, Graybow, and if you ever again come riding into my town like you did today, someone will be carrying you out."

Graybow rode away with yet more filthy words, but both he and his men kept their horses at a respectable trot.

* * * *

Margaret Smith steadied her breathing and tried to calm her racing heart. She'd stood concealed, but close enough to hear each and every word exchanged. She stood in place and listened as Wooly sent his deputies to saddle up the horses for a visit to the Tackett ranch. She waited until the deputies were on their way before she stepped from her cover and approached the lone lawman.

When Wooly looked up and saw her coming, he seemed to freeze in place. It fell to Margaret to say the first words.

"You are a very brave man, Marshal Wooly."

Wooly cleared his throat and made deliberate efforts to look her in the eyes. "At this very moment," he said in a voice suddenly turned meek, "I don't feel all that brave."

Margaret's face flushed, but she extended her basket. "I baked you and your men pies. Please consider them a welcoming gift."

Wooly took the basket and stared down at it for the longest time before nodding his head and mumbling, "Much obliged." He then turned and very quickly started away, but made it only a few feet before stopping and turning back toward her.

He took a very deep breath and then seemed to have to pull his words from the depths of his heart. "I wish you weren't another man's woman."

Margaret did not pause long enough to let her conscience interfere. "I wish the same, Marshal Wooly."

Wooly wheeled about without another word and walked away even quicker than he previously tried to do.

* * * *

A cowboy who introduced himself in a friendly manner as Zed Martin went to fetch Ben Tackett from his quarters while Wooly and his men remained on their horses. Danner reminded Wooly that Martin had been one of the two cowboys standing beside Billy Bemo the day they ran him out of town.

"I sure wish you'd have let me shoot his face off," Danner grinned.

"I sure wish you'd close your pie hole about that," Wooly grinned back.

The ranch owner came quickly out of his ranch headquarters. Even before introductions could be made, Tackett invited the lawmen to dismount and relax. He even went so far as to offer a cool drink for both the men and their horses.

Wooly climbed from his saddle and offered his hand while responding, "Thanks all the same, Mr. Tackett, but we won't be imposing on you all that long. I'm CB Wooly and this is Walt Tabor and Floyd Danner."

Tackett shook his hand good and hard like respectable men do. He then offered his hand to both Tabor and Danner.

"What brings you gentleman to the Tackett ranch?" the rancher asked without suspicion or guile.

"As much as I hate to admit it, Mr. Tackett," Wooly grinned, "it's nothing but pure-d ugliness that makes this meeting necessary." He then went on to relay what he learned from his encounter with Stew Graybow.

Tackett nodded his head several times during the telling, and when it concluded, he took a moment or two before responding, "Marshal, I wish I could tell you that I had not hired a gunman, but the fact is I did. If there had been better ways available to me to bring justice to those responsible for Chuck Lawson's death, I would have done it. I now only regret that an innocent man, that being Rob Cotton, died as a result of my dealings."

Wooly nodded several times to indicate he understood. "What is done is done, Mr. Tackett. I don't know I would have acted any different had I been placed in your predicament. Sadly though, my only concern now is for the citizens of Beaver City. If there is to be a war, I can't allow it to be waged in my jurisdiction. I've told Graybow, a man I have no respect for whatsoever, neither him nor his hands can carry handguns into Beaver City. I think it only fair and right I inform you of the same. As I told that old rascal, you and your men can carry rifles between your ranch and my town, but once in town, I expect the rifles to stay in the scabbards."

Tackett nodded his understanding. "I'll respect your policy, Marshal, and will insure my hands do the same."

"This is an unfortunate turn of events, Mr. Tackett. Men on both sides will no doubt end up dead. I honestly wish you and your men the best."

Tackett once again extended his right hand toward Wooly. "As much as I wish it were not so, it will surely in some form or fashion spill over into your town. I wish the same for you and your deputies."

Wooly and his men had turned their mounts to leave, but made it only yards before Ben Tackett called out to them.

"Marshal Wooly, I just remembered something damned important," Tackett said as he moved quickly to the mounted man. "I'm not as young as I once was and sometimes my brain seems older than my body. So, you'll have to forgive me for almost failing to give you this fair notice. Laughing Billy told me he intends to kill both you and Deputy Danner. I believe he means it. Now, I can't say I won't use that man's services again. But you have my word that, should he come after either of you, it won't be at my urging."

"I take you at your word, Mr. Tackett," Wooly said before smiling and taking a moment to chuckle. "Should you get a chance, just tell Laughing Billy to get his ass in the killing Wooly line. As it stands now, he's right behind Stew Graybow."

* * * *

Walt Tabor drew the graveyard shift. It was just past midnight and he prepared to go out and make his rounds when Tiny Ford burst through the office door huffing and puffing. Like most men who sported the moniker "Tiny," Ford was anything but. As the proprietor of the only whorehouse in Beaver City, the more respectable business owners often held Ford in low esteem, but he'd struck Tabor as a more decent type of those who made their living from the skills of fallen women. Something pressing had clearly brought the robust Ford running and he could barely speak.

"Got to get Marshal Wooly!" he gasped.

"The marshal's in bed, Tiny. I've got the night watch. What's got you in an all-fired fit?"

"Two scalawags got one of my girls by the hair of her head and say they won't let her go until Wooly makes a showing." Tiny acted openly frantic and still fought to catch his breath.

"You know them?"

"Drifters that I ain't never laid eyes on before."

"They look like the serious gun types?"

"They got guns, but I'm not sure what type you're referring to."

"How they dressed? How they heeled?" Tabor knew the more capable kind often dressed in a braggadocios manner and took pride in the iron they carried.

"They look like a couple of trail bums to me. They both have cap and ball pistols that look about as well kept as their owners."

Tabor nodded his head and started toward the door.

"You going to go get the marshal?"

"Nope. I'm going to go get the scalawags."

"But there's two of them!" Tiny objected. "They got Lori Jean and she's one of my most profitable girls. I'd feel better if Wooly was to go. I mean, well, you know what I mean?"

Tabor knew what he meant. The look in Tiny's eyes and the tone of his voice referred clearly to Tabor's past.

"You mean you'd rather someone other than a coward go to Miss Lori Jean's rescue?"

"I didn't say that," Tiny stammered.

"You can go with me, or you can stay here," Tabor said as he turned and walked out the door. How could he tell Tiny Ford it wasn't the trail bum types who gave him serious pause?

* * * *

Walt Tabor pushed through the doors of the Ford establishment with both guns in his hands cocked and pointed. Two ruffians of no impressive dress or stature stood at the bar and a pretty young girl swayed on her knees between them. The man farthest from Tabor held her in place by the hair of her head while she wailed out of sheer fright. The few other patrons had pushed themselves into a far corner and anxiously eyed the men and woman.

"Let go of the girl!" Tabor ordered.

The closest one turned a drunken glare on the deputy. "Are you CB Wooly?"

"I am not. Now, both of you back away from her."

"Well, then who the hell are you?" the same man barked.

"I'm Deputy Walt Tabor."

The two men looked one to the other. The man holding the girl then let out a harsh laugh before saying, "Why, hell, killing you won't make us famous. You're no more than just Wooly's coward!"

It presented no simple matter for Tabor to concentrate on the task at hand when two strong emotions now struggled for his attention. One was anger. Men who pulled a trigger in fury seldom hit their mark. The other was fear. Tabor all too well knew the consequences of giving into that demon. Still, withstanding both emotions, his hands remained steady. The only trembling came from his heart. Before saying his say, he took a long and cleansing breath.

"Even just twitch like you're going for those ancient thumb busters and you'll both on this night be sent to hell by a coward. How famous will you then be?"

Once again, the two men looked one to the other and plainly made the unspoken decision to take advantage of Tabor's reputation. They both, there and then, did indeed twitch. And it took no more to set the deputy into action.

Tabor pulled the trigger on both guns twice and both men took two bullets apiece. He'd aimed where he wanted the bullets to go, and that's where they went and, because of where they went, both men died before hitting the floor.

Tabor stood with guns still pointed and didn't even think to holster them until Tiny Ford's voice came from behind and broke his reverie.

"Well, shit the bed, Fred! Deputy, you done clear and smooth took the brains out of both them scalawags' heads!"

Walt Tabor nodded his head to acknowledge the fact as the young whore still swayed and shrieked. Tabor believed it now had something to do with her being drenched in blood and gore.

* * * *

CB Wooly stood alongside his two deputies early the next morning in the preparation room of James Todd's funeral parlor. He sucked on a tooth for a few seconds before remarking, "Shucks, Walt, if you'd aimed at their hearts we could have propped them up out in the street for viewing. The way it is, with the tops of their heads all ripped asunder, they just make for a terrible sight. They'd plumb scare the kids and old ladies."

"Hell," Floyd Danner mumbled, "They plumb scare me."

Wooly noticed right off that Tabor had not taken the shootings in stride. He'd known plenty of men before, who never got where they could take killing lightly. His deputy wasn't frantic by any means. His symptoms probably would not have even been detectable by someone who didn't know him as well as Wooly did.

"Walt," Wooly said as he placed a hand on his friend's shoulder, "if you are feeling down about this, ain't no need to."

"Do you mean do I feel bad about killing them?" Tabor asked.

"Yup."

"I don't, CB. I feel bad because I'm thinking maybe you're thinking, that I could have just as easily winged them like Bardoe was once known to do."

"Why hell, no, Walt, I ain't thinking that. It's always been my belief that if a lawman's justified in pulling his gun and shooting, then he might as well spare the tax payer the expense of a trial, incarceration, or a new rope."

"I'd have to agree," Danner chimed in. "Besides, as it stands, we ain't got no jail to lock wounded criminals in, but there's plenty of room in the cemetery for dead men."

"I could not have said that better my own self," Wooly chuckled. Damn if he wasn't proud of his selection of deputies.

CHAPTER TEN

Getting to Get Down

Olivo had been called Hound so long he sometimes nearly forgot his given name of Daniel. He picked up the name Hound many years before because of his ability to track men and horses on the plains of north central Texas. As a result of the job Boss Graybow sent him on, Hound promptly learned that being able to track a man on the ground didn't do a damned bit of good when looking for a man who kept mostly to towns and cities. Of course, this had never been a tracking job. It was a finding and fetching job, and it turned out to be a job that gnawed on Hound's innards. It wasn't that he thought he couldn't find the man. The problem hinged on the fact that he knew he eventually would.

That fact pestered Olivo for a couple of reasons. First of all, the man he sought was Indian. Olivo, through a series of ugly events spanning a lot of deadly years, had grown to both distrust and despise Indians. Although the man was an Apache, and it had been the Comanche who Olivo had grown to hate, he figured the differences were pretty equal to that between a butt hole and an ass hole.

The other fact Olivo found even more disturbing had to do with the legend surrounding the Indian he sought. To find a man traveling across the plains, Olivo watched for imprints on the ground. To find a man in well populated areas, Olivo turned to asking questions. The things he'd been told about this Apache by all sorts of men, and a few sorts of women, had Olivo wanting to turn and go another direction. In fact, if he had some way of knowing Rob Cotton, Buzz Libby, and Dan Strapp were still up and kicking, Olivo would have taken off for Utah or maybe even California.

What Olivo had been told by whites, Mexicans, and Indians alike, proclaimed that this John Paul flaunted the reputation of the devil, but he truly considered himself to be an angel. A killing kind of angel. According to many of the same people, the Apache could not himself be killed. Depending on who you asked and who you wanted to believe, John Paul survived being shot anywhere from eight to fourteen times and, on three to five different occasions, being cut by knives so long and deep that he should have died on the spot.

Olivo had also been told that if you couldn't see him when he talked, you'd swear and be damned a white man spoke the words. Equally troublesome, the man went by different names than just John Paul. Olivo heard him called Michael and Samael. Mexicans he talked to referred to the Indian as Diabolos, which Olivo learned translated in gringo talk to "devil." Olivo even heard John Paul's Apache name spoken in the native language, but he'd be hung if he could pronounce it properly with his white man's tongue. That wouldn't seem to matter, though, because the Apache apparently never went by his Apache name. Only other Indians called him by the name, and that breed of people didn't seem real sure to Olivo whether they wanted to claim the man as one of their own, or disown him as some kind of evil spirit. Conversations on that particular aspect of the man's personality, had done nothing to warm Olivo to the idea of riding clear back to No Man's Land with John Paul when he did, in fact, find him.

* * * *

Hound Olivo sat on a log and poked a stick at the glowing embers in his campfire. The moon could not be seen in the night sky. Both it and the stars hid behind thick clouds. The flames of the fire only illuminated Hound and a circle of ground of about ten feet in diameter. Outside that perimeter, all else fell victim to absolute darkness

The croaking of frogs and clacking of katydids made the only noises coming from the dark outside the flickering ring of light, until Hound's horse began to whinny and snort from her tied spot about twenty feet to Hound's back. Not overly concerned, he turned to look behind him into the darkness. Like any horse, his mare might whinny and snort at any number of critters, most of which posed no danger to a man sitting and poking a stick into embers.

He viewed a faint outline of his tethered horse, but his eyes picked up on nothing else, and his ears did not detect any sounds not belonging in the pitch of night. Hound turned back and gazed into his fire for a minute or two when he got the strong whiff of cigar smoke. He raised his head to look around and his eyes fell upon a man sitting cross-legged on the opposite side of his campfire. A cigar protruded from the man's mouth.

Hound gasped and nearly fell backwards from his log while attempting to wrestle his pistol out of the holster on his right hip with his left hand. For the terribly long seconds it took for him to free his pistol, Hound never took his eyes off the dark man with the long braids and the derby hat. And for those terribly long seconds, that man just sat watching and not moving as much as a muscle. The fire's flames reflected off two very shiny guns in a mighty fancy gun belt, but the man's hands remained calmly folded in his lap.

With his gun finally out and pointed, Hound blurted with a high-pitched holler, "What are you? Some type of damned ghost or spirit?"

The Apache drew on the cigar before calmly raising his right hand to remove it from his mouth. He exhaled a cloud of smoke and finally answered, "I have often contemplated that possibility. Civilizations throughout history have held beliefs of beings that live forever. I've not lived forever. I am only two hundred years old."

"Are you pulling my leg?" Hound said in a voice still betraying his shock and fear.

"Most certainly, I am," the Apache said with a slight smile. "By the way, you can put away your gun. If I wished you harm, you would now be dead, and if I intend to harm you, that gun won't stop me."

"If it's all the same to you, I'll just hold it a while," Olivo said.

The Indian nodded his head and didn't speak for torturous seconds as he inhaled deeply from the cigar and then exhaled the smoke through his nostrils. "You've been looking for me. I thought at first you might be the law, but I see now you are simply a cowboy."

"That's all I am," Olivo agreed.

The Apache pointed to Olivo's bandaged appendage. "What happened to your hand?"

"A crazy and mean son of a bitch shot a hole clean through it," Olivo said in a voice starting once again to sound like his regular voice.

"Is that why you've sought me out? You wish to pay me to kill this crazy and mean son of a bitch?"

"Hell, I can't afford a man like you, but my boss can. He sent me." Suddenly Olivo found himself once again startled to the point of squeaking. It appeared as if the darkness outside the ring of light had taken form and stepped right up to the fire. Of course, he knew what he saw to be a horse, but no common horse. He considered the possibility of the horse being the devil itself, and if not, at least the very horse the devil rode in on. The animal's coat looked dark as midnight but sleek enough to reflect the flames dancing from the campfire. Olivo would have thought it a wild beast had it not bore a wonderful Spanish saddle heavily laden in silver.

"Cowboy," the Apache chuckled, "meet Cochise. I named him, of course, after a late and great chief of my people."

Olivo waved his pistol back and forth between the animal with the flared nostrils and the man who Olivo dreaded might not be human.

"Surely you do not intend to shoot my horse," The Apache commented.

"Mister," Olivo said with a voice he could not keep from trembling, "you and your horse both got me more jumpy than frog legs in a frying pan!"

The Apache spoke words to the horse in a language Olivo did not understand, but the horse did. With its head held high, it immediately backed away from the fire and seemed to melt into the darkness.

"What is your name, cowboy?"

"I'm Hound Olivo."

"Hound? That's a peculiar name."

"I'm good at tracking."

"You have assuredly done a fine job of tracking me. So, am I to understand it is your boss who wants me to kill the man who shot you in the hand?"

"I work on the Four-Deuces ranch owned by Stew Graybow in No-Man's-Land, outside the Oklahoma territories. There's another ranch owned by Ben Tackett, and there's about to be a range war between the two ranches. Mr. Tackett has already hired him a killer, and now Mr. Graybow wants to hire you."

"How much is this Graybow willing to pay for my services?"

"He pretty much told me to tell you to name your price, and he'll pay it."

"That being the case, I will accompany you back to No-Man's-Land. I'll throw my camp in with yours tonight," the Apache said as he flicked his cigar stub into the darkness.

Olivo wasn't particularly fond of the idea, but it might be best for the Apache to be here where Olivo could see him instead of someplace out in the black of night. So Olivo nodded his head and then asked the only question remaining to be asked.

"What am I to call you?"

The Apache stared hard into the fire for the longest time as if looking there for the answer to Olivo's question. "You may call me Taik-ahi-lahow-dimay."

Olivo sighed hard and crunched his face up in consternation, "Hell, Mister, that name's too long to remember and too hard to say. Are those Apache words?"

"No," the Indian replied nonchalantly. "It's nothing. I just made it up."

Now, Olivo felt truly puzzled. "Dang-it, Mister, I guess I'll just go on addressing you as Mister."

"Too formal. Feel free to call me John."

Olivo jerked his hat off and gave his head a vigorous scratching to dispel his angst. "Seems we could have come to that conclusion in a more simple manner," he exhaled.

"Simplicity, Hound Olivo, would confuse you on the complexity of my nature." The Apache pointed to the campfire. "Reach there and retrieve a handful of smoke."

"Well, hell, Mister, uh, John, I can't hold smoke in my hand."

The Apache nodded his head, "I can be fire, Hound Olivo, and I can, when needed, be the smoke it produces."

Olivo stared hard to see if the Apache had been pulling his leg, but his solemn face showed no signs of joshing.

* * * *

Olivo opened his eyes the very moment the sun popped into his new day. Being an extremely light sleeper, he found it surprising to see John Paul mounted on his magnificent but frightening horse, looking down upon him, and ready to go.

"Could have let me known you was up and about," Olivo said as he climbed to his feet and started breaking camp.

When the mounted man offered no reply, Olivo looked up and into a face deep in thought.

"Hound Olivo, have you ever wondered just exactly who or what you are?"

Olivo considered it a strange question, but still extremely leery of this strange man, Olivo thought it best to appease him. "I'm just a cowboy. Hell, I've always been just a cowboy. I never thought I was anything else."

"You are a lucky man, Hound Olivo."

Olivo wasn't so sure of that, especially considering his present company. He offered no response and continued with his preparations to pack and leave.

"Sometimes, Hound Olivo, I feel I am no more than a white man trapped in the body of an Indian. However, there are moments I endure that seem to mock this assumption. Take for instance my past night of sleep. I had what white men call a dream, but what the People might consider a vision. Whatever one might choose to call it, I awoke with a distinct feeling that this journey could eventually lead to my demise."

"You mean you think you might get killed?" Olivo asked as he walked off to untie his horse.

The Apache spoke a strange word to the stallion and it started to move along behind Olivo.

"That might very well be a possibility."

"But I thought you couldn't be killed."

"Honestly, since my lungs continue to draw air and my heart to pump blood, that is yet to be proven. I've never said I was immortal. I've just never disagreed when others have proclaimed such."

Olivo swung his saddle upon his horse's back and then paused a second to look at the Apache. "Are you thinking you might not want to go with me?"

"Quite the contrary. I'm now helpless to do anything but go with you."

"I don't understand," Olivo said as he removed his hat and scratched a mop of hair.

"To stay behind might mean I will never truly fulfill my destiny. Besides, Hound Olivo, I am the curious type."

"Don't take no offense, John, but besides being curious, you are damned sure peculiar."

"I take no offense to your honest observation, Hound Olivo."

"One more thing, John."

"Yes, Hound?" Olivo noticed this was the first time John didn't address him by his last name as well.

"I find myself acting peculiar as well. First of all, I've said more words this morning than I normally say all day. Next thing is I'm calling an Indian by his first name. John, have you put some kind of spell on me?" Olivo could not have been more serious.

"No, Hound. What you are experiencing is not inexplicable. Those who I choose not to kill, do normally find me engaging."

Olivo winced and scratched his chin on the meaning of a couple of the Indian's words, but he believed the fancy talk simply meant no type of evil hex had been cast. Even though that might be the case, Olivo knew, without a doubt, he'd been thrust in the presence of an being like no other being he'd yet to encounter.

* * * *

Zed Martin teetered back and forth in a rocking chair beside foreman Moose Powell on the front porch of the Lone Star Saloon. The sun had little more than an hour left to perch on the horizon, but the air still felt as hot as just baked biscuits. Martin enjoyed both the shade beneath the saloon's awning and his second cool beer. Powell already put away three shots of whiskey and now sipped on his third beer.

The huge foreman decided earlier in the week he and Martin could have Friday afternoon and evening off for a trip into town, and Shannon Wheeler, Kyle Caldwell, and Ward Avants could have the same privilege on Saturday. Mr. Tackett announced, as policy, that none of his boys should travel alone, and Martin had no problem with it. He also felt pleased as pie to be partnered up with Powell instead of in the other grouping of three. Martin didn't consider the other three hands incapable, but Moose Powell was twice as capable as any two of the other three.

The week ending had been filled to the brim with hard work, and on top of that, Martin endured a fair amount of tension over the brewing range war. As fate would have it, he just started to unwind in the shade with beer in hand when the few cowboys from the Four-Twos who had not been killed or wounded came riding in.

Powell casually pushed up from his rocker and strolled to the edge of the porch to watch as the three cowboys made their way to the Red Bull Saloon across the street. The foreman typically exhibited about as easy going and gentle a nature as Martin had ever met, except when he drank hard liquor.

"Moose, sure is early in the evening to be having to deal with trouble," Martin said in what he hoped to be a calming manner.

"I don't intend to cause no trouble, Zed. I just got a question to ask."

Martin didn't even have a chance to respond before Powell called out to the men who were just then hitching their horses to the posts outside the Red Bull. They'd ridden in all peaceful like, trying to ignore Martin and Powell by minding their own business, and Martin thought it a pity Powell just could not let that be.

"Hey there!" Powell hollered out in a voice loud but not offensive, "I hear you boys have declared war on us?"

Martin watched the three cowboys exchange a few words he couldn't hear before their foreman, John George, stepped forward a couple of paces from the other two. Martin always considered George a serious type with little to no sense of humor.

"It was our boss that did that," George hollered back. "We're just his soldiers."

"So, you'll be doing the fighting?" Powell responded.

"That's what soldiers do," George answered without as much as a flinch.

"Why, hell, little man, there's only three of you. Three soldiers don't make for much of an army."

Martin involuntarily let out a low moan and slowly shook his head. It'd started off peaceful enough. Powell had not tinted his initial question with a hateful tone or ugly words. And, too, Martin had sensed no bile in George's first response, but he could have left out that soldier part because, from that point on, it started getting ugly fast.

George must have taken some offense at being referred to as little because his voice now had a definite edge to it. "Hound Olivo is currently gone, but not gone for good. That makes us four. And when ol' Hound gets back from where he's gone to, he's bringing more help."

Powell had been somewhat slumped against a support pole, but now he straightened to his full height, and Martin moaned even louder a second time.

"What kind of help?" Powell asked with attitude.

"I can't help but think that ain't none of your business," George replied with some attitude of his own.

"Guess the hell I'll make it my business then!" Powell said just before jumping off the porch and breaking into a run.

Martin sat up straight in his rocker, but only to get a better view. He didn't make any effort to stand. He found no sense in doing so. Three to one were not odds Powell required assistance with. As a matter of fact, if Martin jumped in, Powell might just whip him for doing so.

* * * *

Bill Norris's instinct advised to either run or jump. He could run into the Red Bull Saloon, or he could jump on his horse and let his horse do the running. Instead of immediately doing either, he glanced across the back of his horse and into the face of Lester Jiggs. This counted the second damn time in no time at all they'd both been in danger of being stomped by Moose Powell, and the fact showed all too clear in Jigg's face.

"I told him, John! I told him!" Jiggs shouted.

He certainly had. When Powell first called out from across the street, John George asked their opinion on how best to respond to the question Powell asked.

"Ignore him. Let's just up and get in the saloon and act like we didn't hear him, John" Jiggs offered.

"We can't ignore him," John responded.

"Well then," Norris said, "tell him that war business is all Mr. Graybow's doings."

John George then took it a bit further than Norris suggested. Now, one very big and strong and whiskey-mean kind of man bore down on George, and George had to take up a fighting stance.

"John ain't running!" Jiggs hollered at Norris just before cupping a hand to his mouth and turning back toward George, "Run, John! Run!"

As if stuck in a wagon rut, Jiggs turned again to Norris, "John ain't running!"

"Hell, I know he ain't running, Lester. That means we can't run either."

Some years back Norris passed through New Orleans just as a hurricane slammed into the old city. The memory popped into his mind as a result of how Powell slammed into John George. Norris started for his foreman at a trot, and he heard Jigg's heels pounding the ground right behind him.

Norris could not help but feel as hopeless as a man running up only to piss on a forest fire.

* * * *

Floyd Danner enjoyed a supper of fried chicken just down the street from the Red Bull and Lone Star Saloons when he heard the familiar commotion of men fighting.

"Keep my chicken warm, Charlie!" Danner called to the cook before darting out the door and into the street.

The deputy immediately noticed the very big foreman of the Tackett Ranch. One man already laid at his feet, spread-eagle, and out cold. The foreman had hold of another two men, one in each hand, and he worked them like a set of cymbals. He had them each by the back of their shirt collars and again and again pulled them wide apart and then slammed them back together. It gave the illusion the two men were fighting each other, but at this point, they were only fighting to stay conscious.

Danner stepped up into the big man's line of vision but not close enough to be hit by flying body parts.

"Looks like them boys have had enough. Let 'em go."

Danner issued his order plenty loud and forceful enough, but it appeared the big man didn't hear a word of it. Danner did not believe in repeating lawful orders. Instead, he pulled his revolver and put a bullet between the foreman's spread feet.

* * * *

The explosive gunshot and the sight of dirt being kicked up between his legs didn't bring Moose Powell completely to his senses, but enough so that he realized a man held a gun on him and shouted words in his direction. A moment later he came around to recognize the man as the deputy named Floyd Danner.

"What do you want?" Powell growled while continuing to pound Bill Norris and Lester Jiggs into each other.

"I want you to let those men go, and I want you to let them go now!"

No man customarily took that tone of voice with Powell. He did as Danner ordered, but not because of the order. The cowboys collapsed in a heap, and Powell spun to face the lawman head on.

"Don't be telling me what to do!" Powell bellowed.

"You might just settle down, cowboy, because you're looking like you might want some of me," Danner said as he holstered the pistol.

A rage still brewed in Powell. It had always been that way. Once he started handing out ass whippings, he just wanted to keep on doing it. "If you're thinking that's the case, then a little feller like you ought to keep that gun out and handy."

"I don't need a gun to take care of you."

* * * *

Zed Martin moved up closer, but not too close, and he very much understood the surprised look suddenly spreading across Moose Powell's face. Martin, like Powell, could not believe from the evidence scattered at Powell's feet that Deputy Danner stood ready and willing to take Powell on without a gun.

"You intend to take me to jail without using a gun? Well, Deputy, you best go get Wooly and that other deputy. I'll wait here for you."

"Don't need them. And I don't intend to take you to jail because we ain't yet got a jail."

"Then what do you intend?" Powell sneered as a challenge.

Danner pointed to the three men scattered on the ground. "I'm going to beat you down just like you did them. Then, I'm going to let this man," Danner paused to point a finger at Martin. "carry you back out to the ranch so he can tell the story of what happened here today."

Danner's words had been so calm and matter of fact that Martin almost believed he might be able to do exactly what he said he intended to do. It surprised Martin when Danner turned and addressed him.

"You tell Mr. Tackett that I regretted having to do this, and had his foreman here just done as he was told the very minute he was told to do so, I'd simply sent you two home for the evening. Do you understand that?"

"Yes, sir. I understand." Or at least Martin thought he might. Danner still had a lot of getting to get done.

"You honestly think you can whip me?" Powell spoke up.

Danner turned back to Powell. "Yup."

Then the deputy just waded right in.

Martin could not keep his mouth from gaping as the two men exchanged a series of blows landing like shotgun blasts. All too soon, and to Martin's absolute amazement, Danner started gaining the upper hand. It just seemed to come down to the fact Danner could take a punch better than Powell. In the next few seconds, a dazed Powell began to swing and miss while Danner continued to connect. When it came to the point that Powell's huge hands fell limp to his side out of pain and exhaustion, Danner stepped in and planted a fist which landed like a brick right in the middle of Powell's face.

Martin's foreman stumbled backwards and then collapsed. He hit the ground and did not move.

Only one word passed through Martin's mind and out his lips. "Damn!"

Danner took a few deep breaths and then swiped at the blood streaming from both his nose and lips. "Get him on home," he nodded to Martin.

"I'm not sure I can get him on his horse all by myself," Martin exclaimed.

"I'll give you hand. In exchange, you can tell me how this all got started."

CHAPTER ELEVEN

A Storm Is Approaching

CB Wooly sat in a chair in the marshal's nearly completed office and watched as Walt Tabor treated Floyd Danner's battered and swelling face with coal oil. With each swipe and dab of coal oil on his cuts, Danner let out a sharp yelp.

"Hell fire," Danner moaned, "you think you might try to be a bit rougher?"

"I might if I tried," Tabor grinned in return to Danner's grimace.

"You should have borrowed my club, Floyd," Wooly chuckled.

"Ain't my way," Danner grunted.

"Maybe I ought to teach you to shoot," Tabor added.

"No need in shooting a man I can whip," Danner replied.

"You ever met a man you can't whip?" Wooly asked out of sincere curiosity.

"Came damn close to it today," Danner winced.

Wooly sat back and watched Tabor scrub and patch while considering the information Zed Martin relayed to Danner. John George took his beating without telling Moose Powell about the man Hound Olivo had been sent to retrieve, but Norris and Jiggs began to talk after a half dozen or so times of colliding face to face.

"So, you've heard of this Apache?" Wooly asked Danner.

"Yeah. He's somewhat of a legend west of here. He's a real dandy. Talk has it that he's highly educated. I've heard he speaks like some kind of university professor, but that he's as stealthy and tricky as old Geronimo himself. A lot of what is said is simply too hard to believe."

"Like what?" Tabor asked.

Just a slight tone in his deputy's voice gave Wooly an unsettled feeling that Tabor might be a tad too concerned about just another hired killer.

"Manure kind of stuff," Danner answered. "Some say he is the devil. Others say he can't be killed."

"I don't know of a man yet invented that can't be killed," Wooly added for Tabor's benefit.

"Yeah," Tabor mumbled, "but some men are a lot harder to kill than others."

Wooly decided there and then it had come time to invite both his deputies to his room for a drink, a special presentation, and a confession.

* * * *

Wooly poured three drinks and then passed a glass each to Danner and Tabor. He restrained himself to just a sip of his whiskey. He planned on doing his serious drinking once he sent his men on their way.

"Boys, I'd be remiss if I didn't admit a storm is approaching Beaver City. We don't need to fool each other about the fact that we might soon find ourselves between the guns of two capable killers."

"I don't fear any man when I'm standing shoulder to shoulder with you, CB," Danner said solemnly.

Those words pained Wooly's heart, but he held off addressing why. Instead, he went to his bed, and to his knees, so he could retrieve a box he kept hidden there. He stood and placed the box on his bed and took a deep breath before thumbing open the latches concealing a long-held treasure. He reached within the box and retrieved two forty-five caliber Colts with pearl handles.

With a gun in each hand, Wooly approached his two deputies and extended one to each.

"These belonged to Clay Bardoe," he announced as both Danner and Tabor took the guns in their hands.

"Now they are yours."

It appeared neither man knew what words to say, so Wooly spoke on.

"If those guns could talk they'd teach a lesson about both right and wrong. They'd tell a story about truth and justice and love and hate. They'd tell us about what both makes a man and what destroys a man."

"I can't take this," Tabor stammered. "This is the very reason I threw down my gun and badge. This gun is the reason I'm known as a coward, and the reason I'm here today."

"That's part of its magic, Walt," Wooly nodded. "That's the exact reason you should accept it. You just said it. If it weren't for that gun, you wouldn't be here right now. I think you should take it and wear it proudly, and when you have to, use it to show all who care to see, that you are not a coward."

Tabor stared down at the gun in his hands and slowly shook his head. "That's all fairly easy for you to say, CB," Tabor said without raising his eyes to meet Wooly's. "After all, you're the man who went up against these guns. And you're the man who killed the one who held them."

"I'm glad you brought that up, Walt," Wooly said only after taking a healthy sip, if not a gulp, of his whiskey. He then crossed to the one chair in the room and settled into it. "There's a key part of that gunfight which has never been told because I never told it. Oh, believe me, it happened just like the books have recorded it. Clay let me pull my gun and cock it just like the offer he made you, Walt, and I didn't hesitate a blink of an eye. I shot and I missed, and Clay grabbed those two guns, and I knew I had maybe one good long second to get off one more round. And I did. And I killed him."

"What the hell could be missing out of that story, CB?" Danner asked. "You shot him. He died. End of story."

Wooly raised an index finger to make a point as he nodded his head and continued. "When he asked me to step outside and give him five minutes to decide whether or not he'd let me take him to jail, Ol' Clay did more than just make his decision. I didn't know until after the killing was done and I stepped up close to look at his body, but Clay had emptied both of them pistols you're holding while I was outside. The bullets were scattered at his feet. I shot and killed a good friend, who had no chance of shooting back. To top that off, I reloaded his pistols so nobody would know."

Minutes of silence filled the small room. Wooly stared down at his boots, but the telling of what had long been held inside set free the burden that so long weighed on his conscience. In this case, confession did, in fact, do the heart good.

Floyd Danner spoke first. "Hell, CB, I don't see that this changes a damned thing. You walked back in that saloon when you could have just as easily walked away. When it came to the gun pulling time, you didn't think you could take him, but you pulled anyway. You didn't know his guns were empty. That makes all the difference in the world."

Wooly looked to Walt Tabor for a response, but Tabor would not meet his gaze. So Wooly addressed Danner. "The point is, Floyd, Clay Bardoe let me kill him. Had he not wanted to die, I'd been the one doing the dying."

"You don't know that, CB. You'll never know that for sure. The fact is you're alive and kicking today. That's the only fact that matters," Danner said with a definitive nod of his head.

"No," Walt Tabor spoke abruptly.

Wooly turned his eyes on Tabor as did Danner, but Tabor stared at the floor.

"No," Tabor said again. "If all things had been equal, Bardoe would have won that fight."

"Hey!" Danner all but shouted, "just because you..."

Wooly threw up a hand with the palm facing Danner, and Danner immediately obeyed the order to hold his tongue.

Tabor took the Colt that had belonged to Clay Bardoe and tossed it on Wooly's bed. "No offense, CB, but I can't accept this gift." He then turned and left Wooly's room.

"That son of a bitch!" Danner growled.

"Floyd," Wooly exhaled, "I don't blame the man for what's going through his head, and I'd consider it a personal favor if you did the same."

* * * *

Floyd Danner could not let it go. He went looking for Walt Tabor and found him pacing the floor in the marshal's office.

Tabor looked at him, but said nothing. Danner didn't let the other man's lack of words stop him from saying his piece.

"The very first time I focused drunken eyes on CB Wooly, I knew there was something special about that man. We spent a couple of days together before him and Clay Bardoe got me to Fort Smith and Judge Isaac Parker. By that time, I was damned fond of both those men, but I'd seemed to form some special bond with CB. Because of his testimony, I went to prison, but that was my own damned fault. All the time I was in there, I figured if I ever got the chance, I'd become a damned good friend to the man, and that's where I'm at now."

Tabor nodded his head in understanding but still offered no words on the matter.

"That brings me to this, Walt Tabor. I want to know straight out, when it comes right down to the point where bullets are flying, are you going to stand with us?"

Tabor seemed to give serious thought before responding, "Are you asking me if I'm going to stand against Laughing Billy Bemo and that Apache Indian?"

"Yeah, that's what I'm asking."

"Well, then, honestly, I don't know."

"Hell, Walt," Danner said with no effort to control the volume of his voice, "You stood up to and shot two men to death a short while ago. What is the damned difference?"

The response came quickly this time, "I knew I could take those two. I don't know the same about Bemo and the Indian."

Danner took a moment to calm himself and carefully choose his words. "Hear what I'm saying, Walt, and know that I mean ever word of it. If you got to pull out, you do it now. If it comes to a point that your pulling out puts CB Wooly in peril, and he is harmed as a result, and I'm still standing, I will hunt you down and kill you dead."

Tabor turned a sad look on Danner and mumbled, "If that be the case, you will be doing me a favor."

* * * *

It made Ben Tackett hurt just looking at Moose Powell. In his heart, Tackett felt about his foreman getting whipped like a man might feel when another horse finally outran his very favorite and unbeaten one. Zed Martin did all the talking because Powell couldn't. It looked to Tackett as if Powell's jaw might be busted. The big man could barely open his mouth to even mumble words.

"An Apache Indian," Ben Tackett repeated back to Zed Martin.

"That's what they said, Mr. Tackett," Martin replied while Powell cupped his jaws in both hands and gingerly nodded his head.

"Well, that's a kick in the butt," Tackett scowled. "No other two men did any more to clear this land of murderous Indians than me and that old bastard, and now he's gone and hired a murderous Indian to kill white men."

Powell mumbled something.

"What did he say?" Tackett asked Martin.

"He said, 'special powers,'" Martin translated. "Lester Jiggs said something about the Indian having special powers so he can't be killed."

"I've known plenty of Indians that claimed to have special powers, boys," Tackett said, "but in the end, they all bled and died just like any other man."

"Then we shouldn't worry about this Apache?" Martin asked.

"Zed, anytime a professional killer is sent to get you, you damned well better worry. Having said as much, I hate to send you out in the dark of night, but I want you to saddle a fast horse and head down south to find that laughing rascal. Do you remember the directions he gave to the widow's house?"

"I think so, Mr. Tackett."

"Then take off and go get him, son. Tell him not to tarry."

Tackett then turned to look at Moose Powell and could not help but wince. "No offense, old friend, but how did that man best you?"

Powell mumbled a short sentence.

"What did he say?" Tackett once again asked Zed Martin.

"He said punching on the man was like punching on a rock."

"Well, I'll say this much," Tackett sighed, "if there's ever a rematch, I want to be there."

Tackett took by the vigorous way Powell shook his head he'd missed the one and only chance to watch a fight between Moose Powell and Floyd Danner.

* * * *

Early in the morning Margaret Smith worked at stocking the shelves behind the counter for what would hopefully be a prosperous day. She had the store open for business for mere minutes when the tiny bell attached above the door jingled to announce the arrival of the day's first customer. It caught her off guard to turn and find CB Wooly standing at her counter.

"Marshal Wooly," she stammered, "what a pleasant surprise."

The ruggedly handsome lawman nodded his head several times before finally getting out the words, "Good morning, Missus Smith. It's, uh, pleasant for me as well." Wooly then turned abruptly from Margaret, stepped to a nearby shelf and made a show of looking over the merchandise on display.

"Is there something I can help you find, Marshal?"

Wooly cleared his throat, but did not turn around. "Well, I reckon I just came in to, well, find something I might need or, uh, want?"

"I might be terribly mistaken, Marshal Wooly," Margaret blatantly teased, "but I figure you to be the kind of man who knows exactly what he needs or wants."

The town marshal's shopping act became even more exaggerated as he started pulling items from the shelf, giving them a very brief examination, and then sticking them back to grab something else. The back of his neck, meanwhile, had turned a cherry red, and it took every ounce of control Margaret could muster to keep from bursting out in laughter.

Margaret considered herself no fool, and she knew exactly what brought Wooly into the store at this very hour, and if she didn't take the lead, the opportunity would be lost.

"I hope you will not find me too pretentious or fresh, Marshal Wooly, but I do believe you are here only now because you know my husband is at the weekly town council meeting."

Wooly turned from the shelf to look at the door and Margaret honestly feared he intended to bolt, but he then sighed hard and turned to look her in the eyes.

"Forgive my intrusion," he said softly, "but I just wanted the opportunity to merely look at you."

Instead of a man who had just spoken a sentence, Wooly looked like one who had stepped up too close to the edge of a very high and rocky bluff.

"I do not consider it an intrusion," Margaret replied.

Wooly displayed relief with a nod of his head and then spent long and sweet seconds studying her face like a thirsty man might look upon a cool glass of water, hoping it would quench his unquenchable thirst.

"I don't know that any man has ever shown such appreciation for my face," Margaret said with a smile. She didn't know why, but she could tell by the sudden look on his face that those simple words had somehow given Wooly motivation.

"I'm the one who might now appear fresh, Missus Smith," Wooly started with considerable effort, "but I think you might be the woman I've looked for my entire life. But I fear I have found you only, now a married woman, as my punishment for killing my good friend and partner, Clay Bardoe."

It took Margaret long seconds to come up with a response. She used the time to walk around the counter and come within an arm's length of Wooly. "But Marshal Wooly, what else could you have done in such a predicament?"

"I could have just left town and let him be."

"And left the job for another man to do? Another man might have lost his life doing what only you were capable of doing. How many more would have died had you not performed your duty?"

Wooly looked away from her face for the first time to stare at the floor as he slowly shook his head. "Or, I could have just thrown down my badge and talked Clay into heading down to Mexico with me. We could have lived out our lives down there and he'd never had to account for his actions."

Margaret took a deep breath before boldly expressing a whim, "Marshal Wooly, if I were to pack my belongings this very minute, would you head down to Mexico with me?"

Wooly's eyes shot back up to her face and he came as close to gasping as a man of his caliber could. He then shut his eyes and tilted his chin to the ceiling as he once again shook his head. "I cannot forsake my duties or my friends."

Although a large part of both her heart and mind wished his response might be different, the answer came as expected. Margaret forced a smile and a chuckle. "And neither could you have forsaken your duty to bring Clay Bardoe to justice."

She continued to fake joviality to hush a suspicion that had Wooly answered her challenge otherwise, she would at that moment be packing her bags.

Once again Wooly looked back upon her face and sighed. "Perhaps you are right."

For long and silent seconds, he stood and studied her face and Margaret did the same with his. "Missus Smith, do you think it possible a man can love a woman he has never even touched?"

Oh, but he had touched her, and in a place, and in a way, no man had ever touched before. Margaret raised her right hand and extended it palm up toward Wooly. She experienced neither surprise nor insult when the marshal took an abrupt step backwards.

"One touch of your hand would never do," he said before spinning about and hurrying toward the door.

Margaret knew if she said nothing he would keep right on going. "Marshal Wooly!"

He stopped in the doorway and turned back. "Yes, Missus Smith?"

"I do believe it possible for a man to love a woman he has never touched. It is equally possible for a woman to do the same."

CB Wooly nodded and disappeared out the door with a look of sadness so intense that Margaret Smith feared she would never clear it from her mind's eye.

CHAPTER TWELVE

Just an Awful Type

Stew Graybow leaned against a column on his front porch and watched as Hound Olivo and the Apache approached the house on horseback. Graybow learned of the hired killer through a Mexican whore he kept in Beaver City a couple of years earlier. The girl came to No-Man's-Land from Santa Fe where she worked in a house the Apache frequented. When other patrons of the whorehouse complained about an Indian being serviced by the same girls who serviced white men, the owner had no choice but to bar the Apache from the premises. The Mexican whore witnessed the Apache's retribution on the patrons who had objected and the owner himself. Graybow had never been able to forget the stories the whore told. Nor could he forget the descriptions she gave of the notorious killer.

The man dressed in dark colored finery on the back of a daunting black stallion fit almost perfectly the image Graybow had formed in his mind. He could not help but smile at what his eyes now beheld. Could there be a more terrifying entity he could send sweeping down upon his enemies? Graybow did not believe it possible. No other man Graybow ever laid eyes on could more perfectly personify death and destruction.

"John Paul?" Graybow called down from his porch.

"Stew Graybow?" the dark man called back.

"I never thought I'd see the day I'd invite an Indian into my home," Graybow grinned, "but you and I have special business to discuss."

"I am honored," the Apache said with a smirk, "to be the first of my people to cross your threshold."

Graybow quickly made the decision not to be insulted by the killer's arrogance. If he had no arrogance, he would not fit perfectly into Graybow's plan.

"Hound," Graybow called out to Olivo, "you did a good job and I appreciate it. Now, you tend to the horses and then take the rest of the day and tomorrow off."

"Hell, Mr. Graybow," Olivo scowled, "that stallion won't let me lay a hand on him."

"That is correct," the Apache nodded. "No man touches my horse. He'll stand right here and wait for me and will neither need hobbled or tethered. He'll take water when I tell him."

"Have it your way, John Paul," Graybow said before motioning for the Apache to follow him into his house.

When normally discussing business, Graybow usually offered the other man a glass of fine Kentucky bourbon, but this time he poured a glass only for himself. He might have stooped to let an Indian in his house, but he'd be damned if he drank with one. If the act offended the Apache, it did not show on his face. If it had, Graybow would not have given a damn.

"I need seven men killed, John," Graybow said as he motioned the Apache to have a seat in the parlor and moved to sit himself.

"I suppose you are prepared to pay a great sum to have me dispose of that many men, Stew Graybow," the Apache said as he selected a chair and took a seat.

Graybow took a sip of his whiskey and then looked the Indian hard in the eyes. "I prefer those who work for me address me as Mr. Graybow."

"I don't call any man mister, Stew Graybow. Besides, I won't be working for you. I'll merely be killing for you."

Graybow took a deep breath to steady his anger. "I don't guess it matters much, but I don't think this will end up being a friendly arrangement," he said without doing much to disguise his distaste for the Apache.

"I've never in my life addressed any man as 'friend,' and you will certainly not be my first. Besides, I'm no more interested in being friendly with a killer of Indians than you are in being friendly with a 'savage.' Having that out of the way, can we now discuss money?"

Graybow found satisfaction in learning the Apache knew of his reputation as a skilled Indian fighter. "I will give you two hundred and fifty apiece for killing the seven I need killed."

"You will give me five hundred apiece," the Apache responded calmly. "I learned from Hound Olivo the Tackett ranch has only five cowboys. Ben Tackett makes six. Who is the seventh?"

"I'll go five hundred apiece," Graybow growled, "but only because I said I'd let you name your price. The seventh man is the newly appointed marshal of Beaver City. His name is CB Wooly." Graybow noted the name registered quickly with the Apache, and the heathen showed for the first time just a hint of emotion on his face. It appeared so slightly that Graybow could not give it a title.

"Books have been written about CB Wooly," the Apache commented. "He is obviously a man of skill and reputation. I won't kill him for less than a thousand."

Graybow gripped the arms of his chair and clamped down on his lower lip with his upper teeth to keep from saying words that might both ruin this deal and cause the Apache to turn on him. "When I said you could name your price, I expected you would be reasonable."

"It is my opinion that the price is reasonable, and I'm the one who will have to kill the man. Therefore, my opinion is the only one that truly matters. You can pay me a thousand dollars to kill him. Or, Stew Graybow, you can kill him yourself for free."

Graybow spent the next few seconds glaring into the Apache's eyes and the deep dark orbs never once even blinked. "For the price you're asking, I'd expect this job to be done damned fast," he finally made himself utter.

"How far is the Tackett ranch from here?" The Apache asked.

"Fifteen miles."

John Paul nodded his head and then shrugged his shoulders. "Tackett and his men will be dead before sunup tomorrow. I will need a couple of days of spiritual preparation before killing CB Wooly."

Graybow bent forward and stared down at the likeness of Christ on the cross tooled into the leather of the Apache's boot tops. "Just what God do you worship, John Paul?"

"I worship nothing," the Apache smirked, "but I do occasionally hold session with both the God you White Eyes call Christ and to the God of my people, Usen."

"Two Gods?" Graybow snickered tauntingly, "I would find that downright confusing, John Paul."

"The illiterate types often do, Stew Graybow."

"I think this meeting is over," Graybow said through gritted teeth, "I don't care to see you again until you show up for the bounty."

"That being the case," the Apache said as he stood and started away unescorted without looking back, "then I do certainly look forward to when we meet again."

The old rancher recalled a time when no Indian dare turn his back on Stew Graybow.

* * * *

"Tell me about that Indian," foreman John George said to Hound Olivo through a pair of battered lips that were not yet showing signs of healing.

Olivo toiled at the process of unpacking his saddle bags and bedroll and putting his traveling gear away in the trunk at the foot of his bunkhouse bed. He'd already sunk into an awfully sour mood because Lester Jiggs told him how that crazy laughing son of a bitch murdered Libby, Strapp, and Rob Cotton. Jiggs also explained why Norris, John George, and him were all so badly banged and bruised.

"You know anything about him at all?" Hound asked. George had just strolled into the bunkhouse and the two of them were the only ones in the long and narrow building.

"Just know he's an Apache. A damned sharp dressed one, too. I was out in the barn when you two rode up."

"I ain't never met a man like him, John, and hope to never again meet another. The truth be told, I don't even want to talk about him now, but you being the foreman and all, you asked, so I'll tell you.

"He talks smarter than any man I've ever had to listen to. He's always as calm as a rock. He moves without making any noise, and he talks to his horse in a strange language that the horse understands. I asked him while we was on the way back if that was Apache he was talking to his horse, and he told me it was Latin. I ain't never heard of it.

"The people out where he comes from, John, they say the damndest things about that man. They say he's the devil and they say he's an angel, and they say he can't be killed. And you know what I say, John?"

"What's that, Hound?"

"I say we should have left him back where it was he come from."

"Well, I guess once he finishes up with old man Tackett and his hands and that CB Wooly, he'll be out of here soon enough."

"CB Wooly?" Hound scowled. "Why's he gonna kill a lawman?"

"'Cause that day you rode out, the old man had us all ride into town with him, and he talked to CB Wooly like he might any other man, 'cept Wooly took offense. He invited the boss to crawl off his horse so he could whip his ass. It made old man Graybow look mighty poorly when he wanted no part of that. So, he wants Wooly to pay for hurting his pride."

"I'm a fairly law-abiding citizen," Olivo responded. "I don't cotton to the business of killing a man who wears a badge."

"Well, I ain't partial to it either, Hound, but it ain't gonna be me or you doing the killing. Hell, who's to say that Apache can take ol' Wooly anyhow?"

At that moment, Olivo stopped unpacking. After a few minutes of silence, John George walked away and Olivo started packing it all up again.

* * * *

Floyd Danner sat on the front porch of an all but completed marshal's office and jail watching the sun set when a cowboy rode up and reined his horse to a stop.

"Are you CB Wooly?" the cowboy asked.

"No, sir. I'm one of his deputies. My name is Floyd Danner. Who might you be?"

"My name is Olivo, but they call me Hound. I was a hand on the Four Deuces ranch, but ain't no more."

Danner came to his feet. "What can I do for you, Hound?"

"Don't think there's a single thing you can do for me. I'm headed north of here to try and get a job at the Double E ranch in Kansas. But, there might be something I can do for you."

"And what would that be?" Danner grinned. The man on the horse seemed like the amiable kind of wrangler.

"Stew Graybow sent me out to Santa Fe to fetch a killer. I done did that, and he's here now. I didn't know until just recently that Mr. Graybow intends for this man to kill CB Wooly. I don't agree with that arrangement. I wanted Marshal Wooly to know a terrible man is coming his way."

"Would that be the Apache?" Danner asked.

"That would be him, and he's just an awful type."

"I'll pass that word to the marshal," Danner nodded.

"Then I'll be on my way," Hound Olivo said before starting his horse off with a flick of the reins.

"I'm much obliged, Hound," Danner called after the man.

The cowboy raised a hand and waived a farewell.

* * * *

Floyd Danner knocked at the door to CB Wooly's boarding room and waited for a response. It came in a slur of words.

"Enter, if you be friend!"

Danner opened the unlocked door and announced before entering, "I'm the best friend you'll ever have, CB."

CB Wooly sat in his chair and had a pistol pointed at the broad part of Floyd's body.

"You expecting trouble, CB?" Danner asked.

"With the life I've lived," Wooly nodded, "you always expect trouble."

It seemed all too obvious to Danner that Wooly experienced trouble both focusing his vision and forming his words. A shot glass and a half full whiskey bottle were on the table at his side.

"Are you celebrating a special occasion, CB?" Danner chuckled.

"'Fraid not, old friend. It's a nightly ritual for me."

"I'd be guessing that'd have a lot to do with Clay Bardoe," Danner said as he stepped in the room and shut the door behind him. He'd truly hate anyone else to see CB in this state of near all out drunkenness.

"Well now, it *did*. It surely did. It's bad enough a man has to kill a good friend, but it makes it worse when he's made a hero for the act, and, had the truth been known, there was not a damned thing heroic about the act."

"Once again, CB, I'll have to disagree with you on that statement. You are a hero to me for going up against him in the first place," Danner nodded emphatically.

"Well, I do appreciate the kind sentiment, Floyd, but none of that now matters because I don't think I'm drinking on this night because of Clay."

Danner could not help but chuckle. "You care to explain, CB?"

"I do believe I cleared my conscience when I told you two boys Clay's guns had been unloaded. I believe that, because I didn't need near as much whiskey to make me sleep last night as I normally do."

"Then why are you drinking so heavy this night?" Danner grinned. He himself had been this way often enough, but he'd never seen Wooly jug-bitten, and Danner sincerely got a kick out of it.

"I'm in love with a woman I cannot have," Wooly said.

The lamentable quality of the marshal's confession immediately extinguished Danner's gleesome mood. "Well, why can't you have her, CB?"

"Because she's married to Elijah Smith."

"Margaret Smith," Danner said as he nodded his understanding of how a man might so easily and quickly fall for such a handsome woman.

"Margaret Smith," Wooly said and nodded along with his deputy while at the same time refilling his whiskey glass.

Danner didn't know what else to say, so he just kept his mouth shut and watched Wooly quickly down the contents of the glass and proceed to pour yet another.

"I find it all so tragically ironic, Floyd, that Clay Bardoe didn't care to live because he had held the woman he loved and could never hold her again. Now, here I sit, not caring if I live or die because I will never be able to hold my one true love."

"Why, hell, CB, if you're feeling that low about it, I'll just go shoot that scrawny little excuse of a man. I'll have to get myself good and drunk first, but I'd do that for you."

"I believe you would, Floyd, but I wouldn't have you do that. Don't think I haven't thought about doing that my own self, but murdering ain't no more my way than it is yours."

Danner nodded his head and let go a sigh.

Wooly took in a deep breath and let it out as a whistle. "I feel kind of foolish unloading that on you. So, let's change the subject. What brings you here, Floyd?"

Danner was all too happy to change the subject, even though it was not pleasant news he'd come to deliver. "Hound Olivo found that Apache and brought him back here. Hound stopped in a while ago to say he's severed his employment with old man Graybow because he learned the old bastard has hired the Apache not only to kill off Tackett and his crew, but you as well, CB."

"Why, hell fire, Floyd," Wooly grinned, "that's the best news I've had all day."

Nothing but the whiskey produced those words. At least, Danner hoped that to be the case and did his damnedest to believe it true.

CHAPTER THIRTEEN

Stacked Like Firewood

It wasn't uncommon for Ben Tackett to dream about the days the Comanche ruled over the land he now called his own. There had been so very many atrocities committed. The Comanche did just horrible things to keep the whites from encroaching on their land. The whites committed similar acts just as awful to run the Indians from that same land. Tackett had been both a victim of atrocities as well as one who meted them out. He saw things he could not forget. He'd done things he wished he could forget.

Though they had grown rarer over the years, Tackett could still have dreams like he now had where he could actually hear the cacophony of the crackling of burning wood, gunshots, and screams. But he had never until now actually smelled the smoke.

Tackett's eyes shot open and he sat straight up in bed. This was no dream. Something was burning. The illumination from the flames shined in the windows of his bedroom and cast upon the opposite walls a frantic dance of flickering reflections and bobbing shadows. Thankfully, Tackett could hear no shouting and screaming and certainly no gunfire. He had just enough time to start believing the terrible noises had truly been a product of a dream when one single shot rang out in the night.

His mind came immediately awake, but his old body could not so quickly respond. Long gone were the days Tackett could leap from a bed and spring to action. Instead he'd been relegated to climbing out of his bed and hobbling to the nearest window.

Flames were overtaking the bunkhouse. A distance of nearly a hundred yards separated Tackett's home from the rectangular structure with the low-slung roof, but even from his place at the window Tackett could tell the bunkhouse would soon collapse. The consuming flames lighting the night around the bunkhouse as bright as day, revealed to Tackett absolutely no signs of life.

The old man's heart filled with dread as he realized the single shot he definitely heard would not have been the only bullet fired, but more likely the last bullet fired.

* * * *

Moose Powell could not be deceived by hopes of a miracle nor fear's denial. He knew the air filling his lungs came now from his last remaining breaths. The powerful body he always relied upon for its size and strength was now ruined. It seemed strange to Powell he could feel the heat radiating from the nearby fire, but he felt no pain from the damage his body suffered. He'd already drifted beyond that point. Powell thought it likely his body already died, and now just his mind waited to do the same.

In that mind, while he still could, Powell replayed how the death and destruction transpired, because as bad as that had been, it did not compare to the nightmare of place and position in which he presently lay helpless.

He awoke before the others. Never a heavy sleeper, grogginess did not hamper Powell's reaction. He realized immediately by the smell of the coal oil, that the flame quickly spreading inside the bunkhouse came from a lit and somehow busted lamp. The foreman rolled out of his bunk while screaming a single word over and over again.

"FIRE! FIRE!"

Powell did not waste time or effort trying to extinguish the flames. The fire blazed well past putting out. Instead he concentrated all his attention on arousing the other three men, getting them to their feet and moving them toward the door.

Ward Avants did a fairly good job of getting around on his own. Shannon Wheeler and Kyle Caldwell seemed all but drunk with sleep, and maybe already affected by the smoke as well. Powell grabbed Wheeler by the scruff of the neck with his left hand and Caldwell with his right and moved both toward the door with Avants right on his heels.

Poor old Shannon Wheeler didn't move well on his bowed legs when he didn't have to hurry. Once he got the door kicked open, Powell intended to shove Wheeler out through it first because he'd need the most time getting clear of the building.

Powell gave one hell of a shove, sending Wheeler practically flying out the door. Then the damnedest thing happened. Wheeler instantly came stumbling backwards through the opening as if some invisible force had thrown him back in. Powell caught him and gave him another shove. This time Wheeler's legs didn't seem to work at all. The momentum of Powell's push sent Wheeler stumbling forward to simply collapse on the front porch. He landed in a heap and did not move.

Now Powell had to get Caldwell out and pick Wheeler up. He ducked and went through the door pulling Caldwell behind him and feeling Avants shoving from behind to get out as well. He no sooner tugged Caldwell out on the porch when the man jerked violently a couple of times within Powell's grip and then went as limp as had Wheeler. In a blink of an eye, Avants made it around Powell and headed off the porch when he threw up his arms, spun, and fell over backwards. Although he could not hear the shots being fired for the roaring and popping of the fire at his back, Powell suddenly realized someone was shooting from the concealment of the deep darkness outside the firelight's perimeter.

Not a damned thing he could do about a man or men with guns, Powell kept his hold on Caldwell and bent to grab hold of Wheeler. In the next instance, it felt like some of the fire just a few feet away reached out and ripped a hole in his belly and jumped right in with his guts. At the same time, his legs seemingly ceased to exist. He could not feel them, and they could not hold him up. Powell lost his grip on Caldwell and fell face first on top of Shannon Wheeler, and then rolled helplessly over him, and flipped over the edge of the porch, somehow ending up in a sitting position with his back propped against the front side of the porch.

Powell wanted to grab his stomach with both hands and squeeze at the searing pain within, but his arms were as useless as his legs and no matter what he commanded, they just lay limp at his sides. All he could now do was hurt and stare straight ahead.

Back behind him, only feet away, either Wheeler or Caldwell moaned and called the name of Jesus.

It might have been seconds or it might have been minutes later, when the form of a horse and rider emerged out of the deep dark blackness beyond the fire's glow. The flames reflected off the silver of an ornate gun belt and fancy saddle as well as the shiny nickel-plated revolvers the rider held in each hand. Powell anticipated when the man drew closer, he'd be wearing a bowler and protruding from beneath the small round brim would be two coal black braids.

With both guns extended at arms' length, the Indian used his spurs and mouthed a command Powell could not hear to move the stallion within feet of where he sat helplessly propped against the porch. The sleek and muscular stallion pawed and stomped the ground and snorted as if it wished to plunge forward and finish Powell off before the Apache could do so.

The dark man in the fancy clothes stared down into Powell's eyes. The look on his face offered no emotion whatsoever, no glut of victory, no hate for a downed enemy, no remorse for four lives destroyed. He then turned his eyes from Powell to stare at the doorway of the bunkhouse and the fire roaring within. When he spoke, his voice sounded calm and as emotionless as the expression on his face.

"There should be one more. Where is he?"

"Zed Martin," Powell mumbled and immediately felt stupid and like a traitor for speaking. Forcing himself quickly to think beyond his pain and fear, Powell then tried to redeem his thoughtless blunder. "He quit. Rode out. Headed back east."

The Apache gave the response lengthy consideration before finally nodding his head and holstering both pistols. He removed a lariat from the front jockey of his saddle, formed a loop, and moved his horse the few steps to where Ward Avants had fallen. The cowboy came to rest with his right elbow jammed into the ground so the forearm and hand were in the air. The Apache dropped his loop over the hand, pulled tight the slack and ordered the horse to drag Avants to a cleared place a safe distance from the burning bunkhouse.

After the Indian worked his rope free from Avants' hand, he pulled his pistol with his right hand and put a bullet in Avants' forehead. Within minutes, the assassin dragged Caldwell over next to Avants' body. Caldwell too got treated with a bullet to the head. It appeared to Powell those two died long before the Apache shot them again, but such would not hold true for Shannon Wheeler.

The Apache's lasso flew right past Powell's head and landed around one of Wheeler's booted ankles. When the horse started backing, Wheeler's body brushed alongside Powell's and flopped to the ground next to Powell's feet. The foreman lowered his eyes to discover Wheeler looking back and maintaining eye contact as he was pulled away from the porch. The bowlegged old cowpoke looked just barely conscious, but he had enough strength to call out.

"He's helping us, Moose! He's pulling us away from the fire!"

"You're right, Shannon. You damn sure are," Powell said with a forced smile. When his old friend soon found out the truth, Powell assured himself, he would not have long to dread it.

The Apache pulled Wheeler right up on top of Avants and Caldwell and thankfully did not tarry before putting a bullet in his head. Powell closed his eyes because he did not care to see the men he'd been close to stacked like fire wood. Seconds later he felt the loop of the lasso fall across his shoulders and tighten around his neck. He had gasped for air but drew none as the horse drug him across the ground like a large sack of potatoes.

The choking pressure of the lasso did not fall away until Powell was pulled atop of and lain out on his belly across the body of Shannon Wheeler. Because he could not move, he fell helpless to do any more than stare into the dead and gaping eyes of Kyle Caldwell's face looming mere inches from his own.

These were indeed Moose Powell's last remaining breaths, and because of place and position, he felt thankful for the fact as he waited for the final bullet to be fired.

* * * *

Ben Tackett took only enough time to pull on a pair of breeches and his boots. He grabbed his old, but well-maintained, cap and ball Colt from the table beside his bed before limping out of his bedroom and toward the staircase.

He struggled halfway down the stairs but every step he took limbered his knees, hips and lower back to make the next step just that much quicker and easier to take. As he approached the last few steps, Tackett moved faster down the stairs than what he believed wise or safe, but men who meant a hell of a lot to him could very well be lying in need. He extended a foot downward to take the step that would put him on the first-floor landing when the shape of a man swung from the darkened side of the banister and thrust an extended leg in his path.

The tripping action took Tackett's lead leg completely out from under him. His momentum carried him flying several feet in the air before he landed hard and face down on the oak planked floor. He instinctively threw his hands out in front of him to break the fall, but they did little good and the collision of his right hand on the hardwood floor served only to dislodge the pistol from his grip to send it skidding well out of his reach. His face banging off the floor left him dazed, and the fall knocked the air from his lungs. Momentarily, he could do no more than flop on the floor and gasp for oxygen. He did not get a stable breath before his attacker thrust a boot beneath his belly and used it to roll him over on his back.

A dark figure knelt beside Tackett on one knee and gently pressed the barrel of a nickel-plated revolver to his chest and applied just enough pressure to hold him in place. The man said and did nothing more until Tackett caught his breath and managed to speak.

"My boys?" Tackett gasped.

"All dead," the man beside him responded simply as a fact without pride or guilt.

"You are the Apache," Tackett managed.

"I am."

"Graybow has won," Tackett moaned.

"Seemingly so. At least on this plane of existence."

It was clearly over. His men were dead, and it was his fault. Ben Tackett chose to say nothing more. The Indian seemed to sense as much.

"When I deem a man evil, I shoot him through both eyes. Your first concerns were not for yourself, but for those in your charge. I think you have a good heart. I will put a bullet through that heart, so it need not further suffer for the death of your men."

Ben Tackett closed his eyes and never voluntarily opened them again.

CHAPTER FOURTEEN

That Ass Whipping

In late afternoon Zed Martin rode into a clearing containing a shabby little cabin. Martin couldn't absolutely identify this as the cabin he sought, but a freshly covered grave situated mere feet from the front door made him think it very well could be. Two large, swollen, and decomposing dogs lay not six feet on the other side of the new grave. With all the signs of recent death, Martin figured this to be the place to find Laughing Billy Bemo.

"Laughing Billy," Martin called out, "this is Zed Martin from Mr. Tackett's Ranch. Are you in there?"

The rickety door creaked open just an inch or so for just a second or two before it swung wide open and Laughing Billy Bemo stepped through the doorway with a Remington in each hand, but down alongside his legs. The guns were not, however, the first thing drawing Martin's attention.

"Damn! Laughing Billy," Martin exclaimed with no small degree of disgust, "you're buck ass naked!"

Bemo laughed his laugh as jolly as ever. "The widow woman stripped me down the minute I walked back through her door last week, and she ain't let me pull my drawers back on since! Hell, climb off that horse and come on in here, Zed Martin."

Martin remained in his saddle. "I'd just as soon wait until you get back in your clothes if it's all the same to you, Laughing Billy."

"How about the widow? You want her clothed too?" Bemo giggled.

Martin stuttered a second or two before getting out what he intended to say. "A yup, I'd prefer her having her clothes on as well."

Bemo turned his face toward the open door. "Hey, woman! Put some clothes on. We got company!"

To free his mind of the images he both saw and imagined, Martin pointed to the mound of freshly turned dirt. "Who'd that be?"

"Damnedest thing!" Bemo howled. "It was left to the widow lady to stick her old man in the ground up on the nearby knoll. And that she did, but it seems she just didn't stick him down deep enough." Bemo paused to slap a thigh.

"Well, I crawled out of the widow's bed the first morning I'm back and step out here to piss. I'll be damn if right there didn't lay her old man. It seemed his two hounds, those two now lying dead, had gotten to missing him, dug him up, and brought him on home." Bemo was in a full howl by now.

"He'd been dead and, in the ground, just long enough to be both looking and smelling something horrible. Hell, I wasn't about to lay hands on him. I just dug a deep whole right there beside him and kicked him into it. Then, I broke them two damned dogs of making work for me!"

"You just going to let them rot there?" Martin asked.

"Thought I would."

"You got to be able to smell them there in the cabin," Martin guessed.

Bemo turned a quick glance inside the cabin, then stepped a few feet away from the door and snickered in a low voice, "Widow woman ain't hard to look at, but she don't smell all that good her ownself!"

Martin could think of only one reply to that comment. "Laughing Billy, would you please put some drawers on?"

* * * *

CB Wooly sat and passed the time of day with Walt Tabor in the newly completed marshal's office before being interrupted by Bond Porter popping through the door. Porter worked in Dick Thurman's livery stable on the north end of town. The one next door to Thurman's little wooden structure the town folk had jokingly started referring to as "Town Hall."

Wooly initially resented Porter's interruption. Walt Tabor just had not been acting like himself since the night Wooly confessed Clay Bardoe's guns had been empty. It seemed to Wooly his old partner lost a noticeable chunk of the enthusiasm he first displayed for being a lawman in Beaver City. Wooly had not directly mentioned the noticed change, but he planned to after a little more time of just sitting and jawing about things of less importance. But, from the look on Bond Porter's thin and badly wrinkled face, Wooly guessed the conversation with his deputy would have to wait.

"You got to come quickly, Marshal," Porter huffed.

"What's the trouble, Bond?"

"I don't rightly know," the lanky stall hand emphasized with great shakes of his head. "All I know is from my place in the barn, I saw Mr. Graybow and his cowboys ride up pulling a wagon. Next thing I know, Mr. Thurman is running in and he's mightily upset and telling me to fetch you in a hurry. I went out the back way, so I don't know what was going on out front, but it sure had my boss all worked up."

Wooly and Tabor pushed to their feet at the same time. "Walt, go find Floyd. I'll mosey on that way."

The marshal of Beaver City picked up his axe handle, laid it across his right shoulder and started walking north on Main Street.

* * * *

The inside of the cabin smelled strongly of things Martin would just as soon not think about. Truth be told, he preferred the stink of the two rotting dogs over the musky odor generated by two unwashed bodies that had no doubt been committing all kinds of vile acts.

The widow woman put a plate of salt pork and scrambled eggs down in front of Martin, and it proved all he could do to keep from gagging. He'd never been accused of being a picky eater, but Martin had always been damned picky about where he ate.

"You say this assassin is an Injun?" Bemo said before stuffing a fork of his victuals in his mouth.

"Yup, an Apache," Martin nodded, unable to look while Bemo devoured the contents of his plate.

"I think I might have heard of him. Is he a real dandy of a dresser?"

Bemo noisily consumed his food, but at least he didn't laugh much while chewing and swallowing. "Don't know about that," Martin answered, "but I understand he's a mysterious type of feller."

"Yeah, I think I've heard tell of this killer," Bemo nodded as he scooped up the last of the mess on his plate and thrust it through his lips.

"You got any concerns about going up against him, Laughing Billy?"

Bemo busted out in laughter now and pieces of egg and salt pork sprayed the table. "Hell, Zed! I ain't got no concerns going up against no man, not even the devil his self!"

Martin did not doubt the truth of that statement, but he did doubt his own ability to hold off puking another heartbeat longer. He jumped from the table and rushed for the door.

"Hell, you didn't eat a bite of your food," Bemo called after him.

"Can't!" Martin gagged before bursting out of the cabin and into the welcomed stench of rotting dog.

* * * *

It seemed apparent to CB Wooly that Ben Graybow and his hands expected him. They all remained mounted and faced the south just sitting and watching and waiting for Wooly to come to them. From about eighty yards away all looked calm, with the exception of the city mayor.

From that distance Wooly could pick out Dick Thurman because of his town clothes and because only one man paced about on foot while throwing his arms frantically about in all directions. Wooly made it another twenty or so yards before someone from the party spotted him and alerted the others. The mounted men turned their heads directly toward him, but did nothing else different. Dick Thurman, on the other hand, came running.

"It's a By-God massacre, CB!" Thurman shouted as he got nearer.

Wooly held his words until Thurman reached him. The mayor stopped to catch his breath, but Wooly kept right on taking his long and steady strides. "What they got in the wagon?" Wooly spoke over his right shoulder, fearing he already knew the answer.

Thurman trotted up alongside him. "Bodies," he gasped, short on air.

Wooly nodded his head. "Say no more, Dick. I don't want to work myself up in a lather before I reach them boys. I need a calm head right now."

To Dick Thurman's credit, he fell in and walked side by side with Wooly as he slightly adjusted his course to head directly to the wagon. Most other politicians and store-keeps would have faded back or drifted off.

Ben Graybow and his men were lined up to the side of the wagon. Graybow's horse stood out in front of the others by a few feet and the old man shouted down at Wooly as he drew near, "Thought you'd want to know the war is already over, Wooly. And I won."

Wooly ignored the words and did not as much as grant the rancher a glance. He did, however, take a very deep breath before stepping up to the wagon and peering over the sideboards. Five bodies at least two days dead lay stacked like cord wood. Just thrown irreverently and disrespectfully one on top of the other. At the top of the heap were the remains of Ben Tackett. Wooly hadn't known him well at all, but would have liked to. By all accounts and reasoning, he'd seemed a fine and courageous man, and he deserved much better than this.

Wooly stood at the wagon with his back to Graybow and his men. Dick Thurman stood at his side and also stared down at the pyramid of bodies. The striking end of Wooly's axe handle still rested peacefully upon his right shoulder.

"Dick," Wooly said softly, "I need you to clear out of here."

"Where's your deputies, CB?" Thurman asked.

"They'll be here shortly. Now, you move on."

"Oh, all right," the mayor responded reluctantly.

Once Thurman moved safely out of the way, Wooly slowly removed the axe from his shoulder and gently laid it across Ben Tackett's body.

"I need you to hold that a while for me, old hoss," Wooly nodded. He then turned and faced Graybow and his men with his arms hanging relaxed at his side. The horsemen moved about and adjusted their line so it now ran parallel with the wagon instead of perpendicular to it.

"Every one of you men," Wooly said loudly, "is wearing a sidearm and that violates city law."

"As I told you and you can damned well see for yourself," Graybow shouted back, "the war is over. You have no right to further ban us from wearing our pistols in this town."

"The murdering of five men doesn't change the laws of this town," Wooly said in a tone forced to remain calm. "Now, each and every one of you, pull out them pistols and drop them on the street."

Graybow jerked his head left and right to holler out a counter order to his three cowboys, "No man better drop a gun to the street!"

While Graybow averted his eyes and hollered his command, and his men looked back at him as a result, Wooly smoothly pulled his long-barreled forty-five so when Graybow faced him again, he had it pointed at the rancher's midsection.

"If four guns don't hit the ground in just as many seconds, I'm putting a bullet through your heart, even if I have to shoot two or three times to get it done."

"He's bluffing, boys!" Graybow called out.

"Four!" Wooly said and then cocked his hammer.

"You can take him, boys!"

"Three!"

"If we pull, Mr. Graybow," one of the cowhands shouted out, "he'll get you first."

"Two!"

Wooly could see by the look quickly spreading across Graybow's face that the cowboy's observation had suddenly made a whole lot of sense.

"All right, Wooly!" Graybow shouted, "we'll pull our guns and drop them. Don't you get trigger happy, damn you!"

Graybow's revolver hit the ground first, three others followed in quick order.

Wooly then holstered his Colt and pointed an index finger up at Graybow. "Now, you're going to get that ass whipping I mentioned the last time our paths crossed."

* * * *

John George looked to Lester Jiggs and Bill Norris as CB Wooly stepped up and jerked Stew Graybow clean out of his saddle.

"What we going to do about this, boys?" George asked in words he could not calm.

"It's one man on another man with no weapons at use," Jiggs hurriedly offered. "I suggest we don't do a damned thing."

"I can't disagree with Jiggs," Norris blurted.

George, as the foreman, sat now officially in charge, but he'd be damned if he knew what to do.

Old man Graybow stumbled once his feet hit the ground, but he quickly gained his balance and stood upright, but not quickly enough. Marshal Wooly stepped in close and threw a right jab that landed squarely in Graybow's snarling face. The rancher went down, flat on his back, but immediately made efforts to scramble back to his feet.

Wooly stood by allowing Graybow to regain his footing, but he then stepped in close again and threw an upper cut into Graybow's gut with his left hand, followed shortly with a right hook to Graybow's left jaw. George's boss went to his back again.

Graybow wasn't so quick to get up the second time, but Wooly acted just as quick to move in and make contact. This time he used a right haymaker landing like a hammer against the same left jaw that had taken the last blow. Down Graybow went again. This time the old man did a fair amount of wiggling on the ground like an earthworm before finally getting his feet beneath him, and pushing again to a semi-standing position.

Boss Graybow's eyes were all but crossed and blood spilled from his nose and out both corners of his lips. There'd been many times over the years John George had all but despised Stew Graybow for his cantankerous ways, but the man had always paid well and on time. It became damned hard for George to sit and watch his boss take such a beating, and it got harder with every blow Wooly delivered.

Wooly allowed the older man just a few seconds to regain his composure before he methodically started applying a series of right-hand jabs colliding with different parts of Graybow's face. It looked sure to George that Wooly did not put his all in the jabs, but each served to send his boss staggering backwards a step or two at a time. It finally reached a point where Graybow swayed on his feet and just waited for the blow that would send him to the ground.

That was when Wooly pulled his right fist far behind his right ear and wound it up for a final devastating blow. It was at the same time George pulled his Winchester from its scabbard, quickly cocked it, and took aim for the middle of Marshal CB Wooly's back.

* * * *

Wooly heard the roar of a rifle and instinctively looked down to the middle of his chest for signs a bullet had entered and exited his body, but there appeared no blood or gaping hole. He then left Graybow to sway and wobble on his feet as he swirled around to face the cowboys behind him. One of them lay on the ground with blood spurting from the right side of his head. A rifle lay at his side.

Knowing what he would see, Wooly jerked his head to his left to confirm Danner and Tabor coming at a run. Danner still had his rifle up to his shoulder and now had it trained on the two remaining cowboys.

"He was about to shoot you in the back, CB!" Danner shouted.

Wooly turned his eyes to the other two cowboys for a read of their faces. He observed no traces of anger or revenge, but plenty of fear.

"You boys just sit easy," Wooly said calmly.

The two men nodded their heads, but they still had the look in their eyes of a calf at branding time.

Wooly turned back around to find Graybow surprisingly still on his feet, but that's all he was. He looked like a man sleep walking. Wooly put a palm to the rancher's chest and merely shoved him to the ground. Danner and Tabor were, by then, on either side of Wooly. The marshal walked over to the wagon and picked up his axe handle.

"Boys, if you'd do me a favor," he said to his deputies, "pick that old bastard up and lay him out on top of the Tackett men. He needs to spend a little time up close with his evil doings."

Wooly strolled over to the last two cowboys. He pointed his club to the one on the ground. "What's his name?"

"That's John George. He was the ranch foreman," the oldest of the two cowboys replied.

"What's your name?" Wooly asked this cowboy.

"I'm Lester Jiggs, Marshal Wooly."

"Who are you?" Wooly asked as he pointed his club at the other cowboy.

other cowboy.

"I'm Bill Norris, sir."

"Who drove the wagon into town?" Wooly asked Jiggs.

Jiggs nodded his head toward the body of George. "John did. Had his horse hitched to the back of it."

Wooly looked to his deputies. "Boys, if you could do me one more favor, toss Mr. George here on top of old man Graybow. It's his fault the man is dead. And by the way, Floyd, thanks for saving my life. That was a fine and timely shot."

"You damned straight it was," Danner grinned.

Wooly chuckled and then looked back up at Jiggs and hitched a thumb over his shoulder at the wagon. "Did you boys have a hand in all that killing, or did the Apache do it all by himself?"

"He did it all by himself, Marshal Wooly, and that's the God honest truth," Jiggs answered.

"Where's that Apache now?"

"We picked those dead men up at the Tackett ranch this morning, and he was there when we left."

"When's he coming after me?" Wooly asked.

Norris turned his head and stared away. Jiggs dropped his eyes to look at his saddle horn. Both men seemed suddenly uncomfortable if not a little ashamed.

"I don't know nothing about that business, Marshal Wooly, nor do I care to," Jiggs finally admitted.

"Jiggs," Wooly said with a nod, "do you feel like business between you and me is settled?"

"I do, Marshal."

"How about you, Norris?"

"Yes, sir, I certainly do, too."

"Okay. You two seem to me to be a decent enough type, so I expect you to do the decent thing. You get Mr. Tackett and his men back on the Tackett ranch, and give them a proper burial. Can I trust you to do that?"

"You got my word, Marshal Wooly," Jiggs nodded.

"Mine, too," Norris agreed.

"Well, you boys jump down and pick up your guns. Leave the guns of the foreman and the old bastard right where they lay. I intend to keep them as souvenirs. And one more thing."

"Yeah, Marshal?" Jiggs asked rather wearily.

"If you see that Apache again, tell him if I spot him before he does me, I'm going to cut his head off, and mount it in my new marshal's office. Then I'm going to feed his body to the pigs."

CHAPTER FIFTEEN

Bitter Tears

Floyd Danner found Walt Tabor standing at the bar in the Lone Star Saloon. Only Tabor and the owner, Don Stroud, occupied the saloon.

"You drinking alone, lawman?" Danner grinned.

"I am unless you intend on joining me," Tabor mumbled.

"I do so intend! Bring me a whiskey, Mr. Stroud," Danner said with a wink at the man behind the bar.

"Your first one's on the house, Deputy Danner," Stroud said with his pock marked face breaking into a grin.

Because Stroud acted jovial, Danner deduced he did not yet know practically his entire customer base had been decimated. The fact pricked Danner's conscience.

"I appreciate the hospitality, Mr. Stroud, but I'll hold that offer in the bank for one day when I'm short on funds."

Stroud did not argue with a man wanting to give him money. When he stepped away to fetch a glass, Tabor shook his head sadly.

"I turned down the offer as well," Tabor said. "I fear the man and his business will soon fall on hard times."

Once Danner had his drink and paid for it, he said to Tabor, "Let's move to a table."

Once seated, Tabor seized the initiative. "Guess you're wondering why I didn't take that shot."

"Did kind of cross my mind," Danner smiled. "I mean being how you're faster than lightening and can shoot the teats off a flat-chested gnat."

"The truth is a sad one. I had my eyes on CB whipping Graybow. If you hadn't been by my side, CB would surely be dead. I can't tell you why I'd make a greenhorn mistake like that, but it bothers me something terrible."

"Well, don't be too hard on yourself," Danner chuckled. "I hear tell Jesus was the only lawman that never made a mistake."

"I didn't know Jesus wore a badge," Tabor grumbled.

"It's a little-known fact," Danner winked, but then grew serious. "You've been kind of down in the dauber here lately, Walt."

"That I have, Floyd."

"You could not help but observe the old man stood by himself against four armed men. If there'd been ten, he'd done the same."

"What's your point?"

"I kind of figure you've been somewhat disappointed in the fact that Bardoe's guns were empty. I fear you might have been thinking it makes CB less than what you thought he might be."

"You could not be any more mistaken, Floyd. The only one I'm disappointed in is me. If you must know the truth, I'll admit it. I'm damned scared of the possibility of facing either Laughing Billy or the Apache. I grow even more worried thinking we may have to face both at the same time."

"Well, Walt, that begs the question. What do you intend to do about this fear?"

"Looks like I got two choices. If it comes to a showdown with those killers, I can stand and maybe die, or I can run. In that case, you'll kill me. If that threat still stands."

Danner swilled the remaining liquor in his glass. "I like you. I truly do. But the sad truth is, that is not a threat. It's a God-awful promise."

* * * *

He felt as if he'd been rudely awakened after a snot-slinging drunk. The fact being, though, he hadn't been snot-slinging drunk in years. His entire body hurt something terrible, and the unusual sensation of being bounced about intensified the pain. On top of that, something smelled to high heavens.

Stew Graybow opened his eyes to stare into the purple and swollen face of Ben Tackett. Graybow sat up in the back of the wagon and bellowed a string of profanities. He heard the voice of Bill Norris ordering the team of horses to stop. Lester Jiggs then rode up alongside the wagon.

"I begin to fear you was dying, Mr. Graybow," Jiggs said without looking him in the eyes.

"Why in the hell am I lying on top of these dead men?" Graybow thundered.

"Well, sir, John George's dead body was on top of you, but we pulled him off and laid him to the side."

"George is dead?"

"Yes, sir. Deputy Danner shot him clean through the head."

Graybow located George and confirmed him certainly dead. He then looked about the countryside and asked the obvious. "Where in blue blazes are we headed?"

"To the Tackett ranch to bury Tackett and his boys."

"Why the hell you going to do that?" Graybow thundered.

"I gave Marshal Wooly my word that I would," Jiggs nodded.

"I did the same, Mr. Graybow," Norris called out.

"Why the hell did you do that?" Graybow thundered even louder.

"Because I feared if I didn't, he'd do to me what he did to you, or worse," Jiggs blurted.

"Me, too, Mr. Graybow!" Norris chimed in.

"Well, I don't give a damn if you did give your word. You ain't burying these sons of bitches!"

"It was my word, Mr. Graybow," Jiggs said defiantly, "and I do give a damn."

"Same here, Mr. Graybow!" Norris chorused.

"You dig their graves, you no longer work for me," Graybow threatened.

"No disrespect intended," Jiggs said solemnly, "but I'd just as soon not have to do the work of six cowboys anyhow."

"Me either, Mr. Graybow!"

Graybow pushed himself away from the dead and climbed out of the wagon. He unhitched his horse and struggled up and into the saddle.

"I'm riding ahead to try and catch the Apache. Where's my pistol?"

"Marshal Wooly kept it as a souvenir," Jiggs all but snickered.

"That dirty son of a whore!" Graybow shouted before putting spurs to his horse and tearing off for what used to be Ben Tackett's ranch.

* * * *

Graybow rode up to Tackett's ranch house to find the Apache comfortably settled in a rocker on the front porch sipping whiskey and smoking a cigar. The very sight of such had the effect of sprinkling coal oil on smoldering embers.

"You look as if you own the damned place," Graybow hollered as he reined his horse to a stop next to the porch.

The Apache took a long and thoughtful looking drag off the cigar and then blew smoke forcibly at Graybow before responding, "The place might be mine. I could have already deemed it so in my mind. And what could you do about it if I did, Stew Graybow?"

"Don't push me, Apache. I ain't in no mood," Graybow hissed.

The Apache performed a flicking motion with his hand as if shooing off a fly. "I find it hard to take serious a man who hires another man to do his killing."

Graybow came dangerously close to grabbing for the Winchester in his scabbard in an effort to display for this arrogant heathen his Indian killing skills. The problem was the Apache's hands were a lot closer to his Smith and Wesson revolvers than Graybow's was to the stock of his rifle.

"By the way, Stew Graybow, you have the appearance of a man who fought, and lost most miserably. Who possibly could have given such a famed Indian fighter so merciless of a beating?"

Graybow could not help but being near the point of a slobbering fit. "You know who the hell did this to me! The only reason he could is because he's still alive! The only reason he's still alive is because you are sitting here drinking and smoking like a privileged white man!"

The Apache cocked his head and stared intently into Graybow's eyes, but a twitch of his lips suggested a near smile. "I cannot argue with a word of that."

"When are you going to kill him?" Graybow ranted as if he'd all but gone mad.

"That is a fair question to ask, but, alas, I have no answer. As you so aptly put it, I do have tendencies to act more white than Apache, but I am still plagued with some of the People's ways and curses. I've had 'visions' of this man Wooly, and another man, I cannot identify. They both present me with grave concerns."

"By God!" Graybow nearly foamed at the mouth, "You are afraid!"

"If a lion or a grizzly was to pounce upon this porch, Stew Graybow, I'd be very much afraid, but I would still kill them. I have no qualms in admitting I do fear CB Wooly and this other man I vaguely see in my dreams. Yet, I suppose what makes me feel sometimes more white than Indian is I possess a magnificent degree of greed. Fear alone will not stop me from collecting a thousand-dollar bounty."

"So? Again I ask, when the hell are you going to kill him?"

"When I get damned good and ready."

Lester Jiggs and Bill Norris could not have picked a better moment to ride into view because Graybow had run clean out of what little patience he had to begin with. If a diversion had not been offered, he very well could have said words that might have ended up killing him.

Norris veered off in the wagon to the right toward the barnyard pasture, but Jiggs rode on up to the porch.

"Mr. Apache, I have a message for you from Marshal CB Wooly," Jiggs said with some noticeable degree of apprehension.

"Not now, Lester!" Graybow barked. Although he had no knowledge of the message, he didn't need something being passed that might even further delay the Indian from acting.

"I'll accept the message," the Apache countered.

"Well, now, you keep in mind," Jiggs started, "that these are his words and it's only my mouth repeating them."

"Messages do often work that way, cowboy. What is the message?"

"Marshal Wooly says if he sees you before you see him, he's going to cut your head off and mount it in his office, and then throw your body to the pigs."

"Go away, Jiggs," Graybow grumbled. Once he had, Graybow addressed the Apache.

"I guess you're more scared now than ever."

The Indian struck a match and before applying the flame to the tip of his cigar, he said, "Now, you go away, Stew Graybow, and do it quickly."

The old rancher had lost his patience, but it now looked all too apparent the Apache had lost his sense of humor. Graybow gave him a snarl, but spurred his horse nonetheless.

* * * *

Their routine consisted of Elijah Smith tending the store the last two hours of the day and caring to the closing, while Margaret retired to their quarters above the store to prepare their supper. This particular evening, she placed their meal on the table just as Elijah came through the door in a state of excitement.

"Your prophecy has partly come true, dear wife," Elijah babbled. "There has definitely been bloodshed in our streets!"

Elijah repeated the tale he'd just been delivered by one of many of the town's criers. Margaret listened intently as her husband revealed that the men of the Tackett ranch were no more. She felt her insides clinch and hoped it did not overly show on her face as he explained how CB Wooly stood down Ben Tackett and three of his cowboys, and about Deputy Danner shooting one of the cowboys in the head. The unfortunate cowboy surely bled in the streets, and so did Stew Graybow at the skilled hands of Marshal Wooly. Although she did not revel at the cowboy's death or Graybow's beating, she felt greatly relieved to learn no harm had been done to Wooly, even though he'd come dangerously close to being shot in the back. Margaret just started to breathe easier when Elijah told her the rest.

"As you so professed, Margaret, I do fear there will be more bloodshed in our city. The Apache that killed Tackett and his men is shortly coming after CB Wooly. That killer, Laughing Billy Bemo, has vowed to do the same. I dread, although he be a fine man and capable fighter, Marshal Wooly may not be long for this world."

Margaret Smith let go of the plate of fried potatoes in her hand and it shattered on the floor at her feet. She could not keep from her face an expression that told more than she wished told. A sad and knowing look suddenly erupted on Elijah Smith's face.

"You are smitten with CB Wooly, aren't you?" he mumbled dejected and sullen.Margaret turned and hurried to the bedroom where she shed bitter tears for all involved.

* * * *

Zed Martin and Laughing Billy Bemo did not come upon the abandoned sod house a moment too soon. Lightening danced in the skies all about them and the thunder boomed like cannon fire directly above their heads. Water just started to fall in large random drops, but the bottom looked apt to fall out of the heavens and the rain would be punishing. Martin got his horse unsaddled and hobbled quicker than Bemo and so set about searching for anything around the old homestead that might be used to start a fire in the soddy's fire pit. Once Bemo had tended his horse, he hurriedly pitched in to help with the gathering. Their search produced meager but sufficient findings, and both men were tucked away in the sod house before hard blowing sheets of rain began to pound the one-time prairie settlement.

The widow woman had packed them off with a sack of biscuits, smoked ham, and hard-boiled eggs. After being in the saddle all day without a bite to eat, and sitting many miles from the foul-smelling cabin, Martin had no qualms about eating her food. He pulled his coffee pot out of a saddle bag and soon enough Martin and Bemo were eating well and sipping hot coffee.

"Eating these biscuits kind of makes me miss the woman," Bemo laughed.

Martin kicked back and listened as his trail mate went on and on about the woman he left behind. Bemo talked in such a relaxed and open manner Martin thought it might be okay to just go ahead and ask a question that tormented him something awful.

"Laughing Billy, did you kill that woman's husband?"

Bemo laughed long and hard before replying, "Hell, Zed, I told you he was already dead when I dug that grave there by the cabin."

"I know you told me that," Martin nodded, "but you didn't tell me how he ended up dead in the first place. Did you kill the man?"

"Yeah," Bemo guffawed, "I did, but it ain't what you're thinking. It was a mercy killing!"

"Mercy killing?" Martin frowned.

"Sure as hell was," Bemo giggled. "The man was in a state of torment when I put him out of his misery."

"Was he consumed with illness?" Martin asked.

"Not exactly. You see, I'd just kicked him out of his own house and made him wait outside while I got carnally familiar with his wife. But, you got to understand, Zed, it was only at her insistence. When I came out of the cabin, the man was in just an awful state of discomfort. I merely gave him some relief!"

"Why, Laughing Billy, you might shoot me for saying so, but that is the lowliest thing I've ever heard of a man doing," Martin said with sad shakes of his head.

"Hell, I've done lowlier deeds than that," Bemo laughed.

Martin thought about telling Bemo, if that be the case, he damned sure shouldn't brag about it, but he didn't want to push his luck any further than he'd already pushed it. No words passed for several minutes while the two men sipped their coffee and listened to the rain splattering on the hard-packed sod roof.

"I just might marry the widow," Bemo said all of sudden. "What'd you think about that, Zed?"

"Might just be the decent thing to do, Laughing Billy," Martin replied after some consideration. Then out of shear curiosity he asked, "Have you ever had a wife?"

"Had one," Bemo confirmed. "The poor thing died while with child."

"That's a hard blow for a man to be dealt. Could be the reason you do things other men would find detestable," Martin deduced.

Bemo laughed harder than even he normally did. "Could be, Zed."

Another spell of silence passed before Bemo asked a question. "You ever took a bride, Zed?"

"Nope. Women scare me."

Martin had expected Bemo to find that funny, and he did. After his fit of laughter, Bemo said, "I didn't figure you for being one much a fear'd of anything, Zed."

"Well, that surprises me, Laughing Billy, 'cause I'm a fear'd of many things. As a matter of fact, I ain't just real comfortable with bunking tonight in such tight quarters with a man that takes killing so lightly." Learning the widow woman became a widow woman because Bemo killed her husband after committing adultery just seemed to plug Martin's gullet.

Bemo just barely snickered. "Well, surely, Zed, you ain't thinking I'd do you no harm. Are you?"

"A thinking man can't help but think of the possibilities of such, Laughing Billy."

"You can stop right now thinking any such nonsense, Zed. First of all, no one's offered me money to do you harm. Secondly, you ain't got a possession one I'd care to kill you for, and thirdly, I can never remember meeting any man I was more partial to than I am you."

Martin did not feel particularly honored, nor did he share the sentiment. However, he did not feel obliged to pass that information on to Laughing Billy Bemo.

CHAPTER SIXTEEN

Lightening Or Fire

For nearly two days, Margaret Smith fought off her impulses to run to CB Wooly and beg him to get on his horse and ride hard for someplace, anyplace, far from Beaver City. She had not done so because she knew the famed marshal would not run, and she sincerely did not desire to cause Elijah any additional torment by having further contact with Wooly. Margaret may very well have wished she'd never taken her vows, but the stone hard fact revealed that she had, and she did not take any oath or vow lightly.

Her husband had not yet again even mentioned CB Wooly. There had been neither accusations nor confrontations, and Elijah had not done what Margaret most expected him to do, which was sulk. Instead of wallowing in self-pity, Elijah had surprisingly been on his best behavior, and Margaret grew more than a little impressed when he displayed a degree of dignity she did not know he even possessed.

Although life with Elijah since the night of the revelation had been tolerable, Margaret found living with herself much more difficult. It proved torturous not wanting what she had, and not having what she wanted. She swayed to and fro between guilt and a sense of being cheated. Worst of all, she regretted having spoken words so few weeks back that could now come true on any given day.

"Elijah, a man like CB Wooly will attract other deadly men if for no other reason than to shoot him down."

If her words were, indeed, to come true, Margaret feared she would never be able to convince herself her utterance had not somehow cursed CB Wooly's short stay in *"Blood City"*

* * * *

Upon riding into the ranch headquarters, Zed Martin turned his eyes out of habit to locate the bunkhouse that had been his home for a number of years. Instead of the long and narrow building, it shocked him to find a heap of charred ruins. His eyes then darted to take in the rest of the headquarters' grounds and did not at all like what he saw, or didn't see.

"Something is bad wrong, Laughing Billy. Nothin's moving. It's dead quiet."

Martin then heard the distinct sound of a screen door slamming shut and quickly wheeled his horse to face the only structure on the grounds with a screen door. Bemo was already looking at the big ranch house and spoke the words Martin had just begun to think.

"There stands what's wrong, Zed."

They sat too far off to see the man clearly, but close enough to tell he dressed entirely in black. "The Apache?" Martin exhaled.

"Looks so from here, Zed. Why don't we all slow and careful like move up for a closer look?"

The man on the front porch didn't let them get too much closer before he cupped a hand to the side of his mouth and hollered out, "Which one of you gentlemen would be Zed Martin?"

Martin hadn't even given thought to opening his mouth before Bemo told him to keep it shut. Bemo then cupped a hand to his own.

"Mister, ain't no gentlemen in this crowd. And ain't neither of us go by that name."

The Apache didn't respond. He just stood erect on the porch of Mr. Tackett's house with his hands resting on the handles of two holstered revolvers.

"Let's move on up there, slow and easy," Bemo chuckled. "Best let me do the talking," he added.

"I'm fine with that," Martin agreed.

Martin and Bemo rode right up to the porch before the Indian spoke again.

"I know you," he nodded at Bemo.

"Well, you might, and you might not," Bemo cackled. "They call me Laughing Billy Bemo, and this here is my younger brother, Frowning Fred!"

The Apache looked from Bemo to Martin, but his eyes did not tarry there long. It was clearly Bemo who held his interest. "The cowboy Hound Olivo told me your name, but he gave no description of your appearance. I've had dreams just lately, or maybe visions, of a man with long blond hair the color of the sun, wearing clothing made from an animal's hide. When I said I know you, it's because I know you from my dreams."

"Well, now, just exactly what have you been dreaming about me, Mister?" Bemo laughed.

Martin spent enough time with Bemo that he could read his laughter as well as he could some men's facial expressions. This particular laugh revealed apprehension.

"I've dreamed we will never be friends, but neither of us can afford to have the other as an enemy."

"What the hell does that mean?" Billy laughed the same laugh.

"The way a less educated Indian might put it," the Apache almost smiled, "is that lightening should never fight fire, because neither would win."

Those words didn't make a hell of a lot of sense to Martin, but Bemo seemed to understand just fine because he solemnly nodded his head, and he did not laugh.

"Where is Ben Tackett and his hands?" Bemo asked as if all too ready to change the subject.

The Apache removed one hand from a gun and pointed in the direction of the barn. "They are buried out there in the pasture. All except Zed Martin."

The Apache then momentarily cut his eyes to Martin, and it took all Martin had to keep from expressing both rage and sorrow. The showing of either one would most certainly have resulted in him being shot dead.

"Don't be looking no evil looks at my brother," Billy once again chuckled. "Any man that might cause him harm, would then be dealing with lightening, or fire, whichever you might consider me to be."

The Apache nodded his understanding and several seconds passed before he asked, "What will you do now, Laughing Billy, in that the war you were hired to fight has already been lost?"

Laughing Billy Bemo threw back his head and laughed as if insane. "I came all this way to do some killing, and some killing I will do. I'm headed to Beaver City to rid this world of CB Wooly and his deputy Floyd Danner."

The Apache again nodded but was fast to add, "I've been offered very good money to kill CB Wooly, but he's made promises to separate my head from my body. If I am to go into the afterlife as an Apache, I need to go in one piece."

"Would you be willing to share the bounty?" Bemo giggled.

"With you? I most certainly would."

Bemo turned in his saddle to look Martin square in the eyes. "Brother Frowning Fred," he laughed sincerely, "best you be on your way to do whatever it is you wish to do, while I keep this here Apache's attention."

Zed Martin had no words to speak, but he did nod his appreciation before turning his horse and trotting away for the last time from the Tackett ranch.

* * * *

Deputy Walt Tabor spun at the sound of the opening door and came about with both guns from his holsters cocked and ready to fire.

"Whoa, there, deputy!" the cowboy in the door shouted while at the same time throwing both hands high in the air. "I ain't no threat. I came with good will to deliver a warning."

"Who are you?" Tabor could not control the tremor in his voice, nor did he care to. He'd rightfully been on edge and now took no chances.

"My name is Zed Martin. I was a cowboy at the Tackett Ranch when there still was a Tackett Ranch."

Tabor breathed a sigh of relief, but he did not holster his revolvers. "What is your warning?"

"I was sent to fetch the killer Laughing Billy Bemo. I delivered him an hour or so back at the old ranch house. We were met up there by another killer, an Apache Indian."

"I'm familiar with both," Tabor said.

"Well, I felt obliged to get word to CB Wooly that the two have now become partners, and intend to kill both Wooly and Floyd, and most likely you as well," Martin confessed.

"Are they coming here?" Tabor asked in a huff he could not control.

"I'm sure they are. When, I can't say."

Tabor lowered his guns but did not yet care to empty his hands of their reassuring weight. "Are you willing to stay and lend a hand?"

"Deputy, I don't feel my hand is skilled enough to do anyone any good."

Walt Tabor took a deep breath and holstered his firearms. "Then, Zed Martin, I suggest you ride from this cursed place as quickly as you can. I only wish I could ride out with you."

* * * *

CB Wooly stepped out into the bright sunlight of early morning to find his deputy Walt Tabor waiting at the door of the boarding house.

"Well, good morning, Walt,"

"Ain't nothing good about it, CB," Tabor exclaimed.

Wooly could tell by the haggard look on the younger man's face he'd spent a miserable night performing his assigned duties.

"Walk with me to the office, Walt," Wooly smiled wearily, "and let me partake of this morning's glory before you burden me with what troubles you."

"It can't wait, CB," Tabor insisted.

"If it can't wait three minutes, Walt," Wooly chuckled, "then we ain't got enough time to prepare for it anyway."

Wooly walked calm and easy with Tabor at his side. In his heart he knew such luxuries would not soon be again available. At his age he'd learned to cherish the tranquil moments that precede the storm. On top of that, Wooly's head still pounded from last night's drinking, and a few minutes of peace and quiet simply couldn't hurt.

They no sooner made it through the door of the marshal's office when Tabor spouted the news.

"Zed Martin, the last standing cowboy from the Tackett Ranch, rode in late last evening to tell me the Apache and Laughing Billy Bemo have partnered up to put an end to you and Danner and, probably, me as well. They'll be headed this way soon, CB. How are we going to get ready for them?"

"Well, Walt, 'we' ain't going to get ready for them," CB nodded with a warm smile.

"I don't understand, CB."

"I'm not sure exactly what I'm going to do, Walt, but I know what you're going to do. I want you to leave now. Pack up your belongings, and ride on out of here."

"You want me to leave, CB? Why would you want me to do such a thing?"

"Walt, you've become one hell of a hand with a gun. Lord knows I wouldn't care to go up against you, but your heart ain't in this fight. I want you to pull stakes and get the hell out of here."

"Are you saying I'm cowardly, CB?"

"That's the last thing I'd say about you, Walt Tabor. I'm just saying this ain't the fight for you. One day, I truly believe, you'll come across your time to stand and fight, and I believe sincerely you'll give one hell of a showing. This just ain't that time. I fear if you stay here, your chances of being killed or maimed are greater than I'm willing to allow. I care too much for you to bear the burden of your demise."

"Are you relieving me of my duties, CB?"

"That I am, Walt. You are free to go."

It neither surprised nor disappointed Wooly when Walt Tabor first stuck out a hand to be shaken, and then turned and hurried out the door.

* * * *

CB Wooly found Floyd Danner having his breakfast in the dining room of the hotel his one remaining deputy called home.

"Good morning, boss. Pull up a chair," Danner grinned before poking a fork full of fried eggs in his mouth. "Let me buy your breakfast?"

"Good morning to you, Floyd," Wooly grinned back. "I appreciate the offer, but my head hurts this morning and a plate of lard just don't sound all that appetizing."

Danner leaned in close and said in a hushed tone, "You still trying to drink that woman away?"

"It's become a cherished tradition," Wooly agreed.

Danner forked an entire slice of bacon and crammed it in his mouth. "I feel for you. I honestly do."

"I appreciate the concern," Wooly grumbled.

Wooly did accept a cup of coffee from the proprietor and sipped on it to give Danner enough time to enjoy his breakfast before sharing the news that could tend to ruin a man's meal. Once the deputy pushed away a plate practically licked clean, Wooly let the news fly.

"Zed Martin rode in last night and told Walt that the Apache and Laughing Billy have formed a partnership. I expect them to be here sometime today with a burning desire to put us in the ground."

"Desiring and doing is two different things," Danner shrugged.

Wooly could not help but chuckle. "I held off telling you in order not to spoil your breakfast."

"It'd take a hell of a lot more than that to spoil bacon and eggs for me," Danner grinned.

"I do swear, Floyd, you are as cool as winter rain."

Danner shrugged his wide shoulders a second time. "Hell, CB, I just like the odds. Us three against them two puts them at a disadvantage that I find comforting."

"Well, that ain't exactly the case, Floyd. Walt Tabor rode out of town about ten minutes ago."

"That son of a bitch!" Danner growled with fire flashing through his green eyes.

"Now, Floyd, you don't need to go blaming Walt for that. I sent him on his way."

"You did what, CB?"

"Yup. I did. And now, I'm going to send you out of here as well."

Danner took on the look of a man who had just been slapped upside the head with something big and hard. "What in the world are you saying, CB?"

"I caused this situation, Floyd, and I ain't going to take a chance of you dying as a result. I intend to face those two by myself."

Danner leaned in close again. "CB, I mean no offense, but if I do offend, so be it. Do you mean to die because you can't have that woman?"

Wooly tried hard to be offended, but the man sitting across from him meant more to him than any son ever could. "Are you asking me if I'm pullin' a Clay Bardoe?"

"That's exactly what I'm asking, CB."

"Well, I'm going to tell you, Floyd, dying ain't all that repulsive to me because of my romantic dilemma. But, I got too much pride to just lie down and let it happen. If there is to be a fight, I'll do my damnedest to win it."

"And I'll be there right by your side."

"I'm firing you, Floyd."

"You can fire me as a deputy, CB, but you can't fire me as a friend."

"You ain't going to go?"

"Hell, no, I ain't going. And furthermore, I curse Walt Tabor for doing so."

"Your stubbornness is making me sad, Floyd."

"Well then, CB, I suggest you just scratch your ass and get glad, 'cause I'm sticking with you like stink on a shithouse."

Danner's stance did not please Wooly, but there wasn't a whole hell of a lot he could do about a partner he cared for too much to shoot, and wasn't hoss enough to whip.

CHAPTER SEVENTEEN

Killing To Be Done

Stew Graybow stood outside his barn surveying all he owned and wondering just how the hell he could manage it without a single cowboy. Then he spotted the two approaching riders. Graybow pulled his revolver and waited until the two came close enough to identify. After identifying the riders, and particularly because he *had* identified them, he didn't holster his gun. He knew the man with the Apache simply by his blond hair and buckskins, and the betrayal incensed Graybow.

"Why in the hell did you ride in with this bastard?" he stormed when the men were close enough to hear his words.

The man in buckskins answered his question. "Don't be cussing me, you old fart-knocker, or I'll kill you where you stand just for the fun of it." The man made the threat with laughter.

"Stew Graybow," the Apache said in obvious amusement, "I would like to formally introduce you to Laughing Billy Bemo."

"I don't care to know him," Graybow seethed. It was an abomination having this murderer on his land.

"I find that unfortunate," the Apache practically grinned, "because I have solicited the assistance of Laughing Billy in killing CB Wooly and his deputies. If you do not agree to my arrangement, I fear Laughing Billy will indeed shoot you for mere entertainment."

"I have no say in this agreement?" Graybow thundered.

"You certainly have a say," the Apache nodded, "but if you say wrong, you're then a dead man."

"I'm not paying a penny more for Wooly's death than what we agreed upon," Graybow said, because there remained nothing more he could say.

"I've agreed to split the bounty with Laughing Billy. We are here only as a courtesy so you'll know the deed will soon be done," the Apache said.

"I'm riding in with you," Graybow suddenly decided. "I want to watch Wooly get what he deserves." Graybow's face still hurt from the beating Wooly gave him, and he could not yet pull air in through his busted and swollen nose. Considering the money he'd be paying, Graybow considered it his right to observe the killing.

Bemo turned to face the Apache and laughed like he had no sense whatsoever. "Indian, if this old goat gets in my way or interferes in the least bit, I'm going to use him for target practice."

"White Eyes," the Apache nodded, "I think you would be justified."

"Just ten years ago," Graybow snarled, "I'd shot you both dead for talking about me like I ain't even standing here."

Bemo laughed, but the Apache's face took on an expression that might very well have been repulsion for an old man who had nothing left but words. "Go ready your horse, Stew Graybow. There's killing to be done."

* * * *

CB Wooly looked up from his desk and his forty-five caliber Single Action Army Colt with the seven and a half-inch barrel he'd just given a thorough cleaning. Floyd Danner sat across the small office in a chair leaned back against the wall on its two hind legs. He'd crossed his arms over his chest while keeping a leery eye on Wooly.

"I may be heading to the outhouse here in a while. You going to follow me out there as well?" Wooly grimaced.

"Won't be going in with you," Danner grinned, "but I'll be posted outside the door."

Wooly reloaded his pistol and slipped it in his holster just a moment before Marvin Little hesitantly stepped through the open door of the marshal's office. Wooly glanced at Danner, who solemnly nodded his head. Neither found it difficult to figure out why the proprietor of the Red Bull Saloon paid a mid-day visit.

Little didn't seem all that anxious to converse, so Wooly gave him an opening. "You got a couple of customers wishing to see me, Marvin?"

"Yes, sir, I do Marshal Wooly."

Wooly appreciated knowing the saloon owner took no obvious pleasure in delivering this news.

Little continued, "The Apache is doing the talking. That other man just laughs, and Stew Graybow is there, too, but he's allowed he's only along for the show. Anyhow, the Apache said you and your deputies could come to them, or they'd come to you."

Wooly glanced at Danner and winked before looking back at the saloon owner with a grin. "Marvin, I'm more than a little surprised you'd even let an Indian on your premises."

Little turned the color of a ready to be eaten radish. "I don't care to, Marshal, but I don't feel there's a whole hell of a lot I can do about it."

"Hell, I'm just joshing you, Marvin. From what I've gathered, that's one dangerous Indian. If I wasn't in the business of refining dangerous men, I'd leave him be as well."

"I want both of you to know," Little said as he looked back and forth between Wooly and Danner, "I've known Stew Graybow for a good long time, and I'm sorely disappointed in him for hiring another man to do his killing. I take no pleasure in delivering this message, and I wish you the best."

Wooly and Danner both nodded their understanding and appreciation. Wooly then got down to business.

"Marvin, I'd be obliged if you'd carry back this response. Tell them polecats I'll be waiting right here for them, but I'd like two hours to get my affairs in order. Tell them me and my deputies will be sitting right there on that front porch at four o'clock."

"I'll do that, Marshal." Before leaving, Marvin Little took the time to shake both lawmen's hands.

"Deputies, my ass," Danner grumbled once Little had ducked back out the door.

"I like them thinking there's three of us," Wooly replied. "I also like them thinking they have two more hours to wait."

Wooly stood, grabbed his hat and his axe handle and used it to motion Danner out of his chair. "Come on. Let's get this done."

Danner shot out of the chair. "We going to the Red Bull right now?"

"Yup, but by way of Elijah Smith's general store."

Danner shot Wooly a most curious look. "Why we going there, CB?"

"I just happened to be in there the other day and noticed he has a good supply of side by side shotguns. I'd like one to carry into this fray."

Danner shook his head and chuckled. "I guess that's a good excuse as any for stopping in for what might be a goodbye."

Wooly had no reply; besides, saying any more could give away a secret Danner did not yet need to know.

"If you're going to get a shotgun, CB, why you carrying your club?"

"The heft of it brings me comfort, Floyd."

And at the moment, CB Wooly would take all the comfort he could get.

* * * *

Elijah Smith swept the floor while his lovely bride rearranged some goods behind the counter. CB Wooly did not miss the look the man shot his wife before offering a clearly strained but not unfriendly greeting.

"Good afternoon, Marshal Wooly, Deputy Danner," Smith said. "What can we do for you gentlemen?"

It took every ounce of guts and determination Wooly could summon to keep from turning his eyes on Margaret Smith and wallowing in her beauty. He had to clear his voice not once, but twice before words could come, and by then, Danner had already started talking.

"We got urgent business awaiting us at the Red Bull Saloon, Mr. Smith, and the marshal would like to purchase one of your double-barreled shotguns."

Elijah Smith inhaled a gulp of air and expelled it in a question, "The Apache? He's here?"

"Yes, sir, along with Laughing Billy Bemo. It seems the two have become friendly," Danner nodded.

That news brought a gasp from Margaret Smith.

At the sound of his wife expressing distress, Elijah Smith shot Wooly a pained glance, but then quickly turned his eyes to the floor. Wooly then and there sensed the man knew more than Wooly wished he had to know. It did not do his already sorrowful heart any good to know he caused a decent man torturous feelings.

* * * *

Margaret Smith had not failed to see and understand the transaction that occurred between her husband and her passion with the simple meeting of their eyes. The looks on both their faces, along with the word of the two killers there and waiting, caused tears to fill Margaret's eyes. She had her head down and wiped at her eyes when she heard Wooly speak his first words since entering the store.

"Floyd, reach over and hand me one of those shotguns off that rack."

Margaret looked up just in time to witness a sight defying all reason. Deputy Floyd Danner turned his back on CB Wooly to reach for one of the shotguns, and CB Wooly raised his axe handle and brought it down solidly against the back of Danner's head. Margaret let out a shriek and Elijah exhaled an expletive as the sturdy deputy collapsed to the floor.

"Hurry, Elijah," Wooly said as he knelt beside the man he'd downed, "and fetch me a length of your stoutest rope, if you will."

Elijah jumped to do as asked while Margaret moved from behind the counter and within feet of Wooly and Danner. Then she and her husband stood speechless while Wooly set about securely bounding his deputy.

"I don't think I understand what you're doing," Elijah finally muttered.

"I'm insuring a dear and faithful friend lives through this day," Wooly said as he put the final touches on his knots. "I convinced Walt Tabor to ride away this morning, but I could not convince, Floyd. I was forced to more drastic measures."

"You are going up against those killers all by yourself?" Margaret asked without being able to keep her words from breaking with emotion.

For the first time since entering the store, Wooly looked her square in the eyes, but he held the glance only long enough to nod his head. Then sudden and unusually forceful words coming from her husband startled Margaret.

"No, you're not, Marshal Wooly. I'm going with you. I'll stand by your side."

CB Wooly stood and gave her husband an appreciative smile. "I won't allow that. Your place is here, alongside your wife."

Wooly turned upon Margaret a set of eyes revealing nothing that was not tumultuous. "You have an honorable and courageous husband, Missus Smith."

Margaret considered her husband's offer to help and coupled that with his near valiant demeanor of the past few days. She nodded and turned her eyes to Elijah. "I do," she professed.

Wooly knelt down once again beside his partner and placed a hand gently upon his shoulder. "Please tend to his head. Hopefully I did no lasting damage. I did restrict the force of my blow. If I don't return here shortly, please keep him bound until you have proof that the Apache and Laughing Billy have either left town or died of their wounds."

Wooly used his club to push to his feet. He leaned down and laid it alongside Danner's still form before turning and heading for the door. Before stepping through the threshold, he turned and let his eyes bounce between Margaret and Elijah. "I do fully intend to be back shortly, but if I can't make that happen, please give my apologies to Floyd."

Margaret Smith turned her back to the door so she would not have to watch him walk away.

CHAPTER EIGHTEEN

Clay

CB Wooly hurried to his room and removed the box from beneath his bed. He thumbed open the cartridge gate of the Colt Walt Tabor refused to accept and loaded the cylinder with forty-five caliber bullets. Wooly stuck the pearl-handled revolver down the front of his gun belt and turned to leave his room. On his way out, his eyes fell upon the whiskey in the bottle sitting on the stand next to his bed. Two conflicting thoughts fought for his attention.

Maybe tonight, I'll again get to drink from that bottle.
Maybe tonight, I'll have no further use for that bottle.

* * * *

Laughing Billy Bemo leaned back against the end of the bar closest to the swinging doors of the Red Bull Saloon. The old bastard Graybow stood at the other end of the bar just as far as he could get from Bemo, while the Indian sat at a table almost in the square dab middle of the saloon. Bemo would have enjoyed a little conversation with the men he rode in with, although he hated one and didn't particularly care for the other, but getting words out of either had been like plucking feathers from a frog.

Bemo reached with his right hand across his body to the bar and started pouring another shot of whiskey. "How much longer until I get to go killing?" he asked the bartender, Marvin Little, as he poured.

Little pulled his watch from a vest pocket. "It's two minutes until three. You have little more than an hour to wait."

Bemo giggled a response as he squared back around and started the glass to his lips with his right hand. The Apache had not touched a drop. The old man had drunk probably twice what Bemo consumed.

"This one's for you," Bemo laughed out to the Apache.

The Indian acknowledged the statement with a nod, and Bemo felt the whiskey touch his tongue just as CB Wooly with gun raised, cocked, and pointed, busted through the swinging doors at a near run. The consumed amount of liquor did not slow Bemo's hand, but he had so little time to react. Wooly was nearly on top of him in a blink of an eye, and pulled a trigger from less than three feet away. Bemo had drawn a gun out, but suddenly felt as if he'd been shoved hard to his left side. He'd already hit the floor before realizing Wooly's bullet caught him on the right side of his body, down below his ribs.

Bemo managed never to let his eyes once fall away from Wooly as he struggled up and into a sitting position. Although the gun he'd pulled had fallen from his hand, he pulled a second one. Chunks of the bar began splintering all around Wooly as the Apache's bullets tried to find their mark. Wooly fired three times in the Indian's direction before Bemo raised his gun and got off his first round.

Bemo realized the severity of his wound only after taking that first shot. His eye sight started to waiver, and he experienced the darnedest time cocking his revolver and bringing it up for second shot. But the first bullet he'd gotten off had gone true and Wooly stumbled sideways, grabbed the lower left side of his gut with his left hand and then spun in Bemo's direction. The big marshal stumbled three quick steps that practically put him right on top of Bemo. From his place on the floor, Bemo could see blood spouting out of another hole just above Wooly's right hip.

Wooly reached across his body with his right hand and lowered his gun to put a bullet in Bemo's face when yet another slug slammed into Wooly's body. This one collided with the upper right side.

The bullet shoved the lawman into the bar at his back and the shot aimed at Bemo's face entered instead his left shoulder at a downward angle. The force of the impact pushed Bemo over and to the left. From where he lay, Bemo watched Wooly straighten and shoot two rounds in quick order toward the center of the saloon. Bemo's left arm now seemed no good and his right side felt as if consumed by hellfire, but he struggled with his right arm and hand to free another Remington.

Less than a foot of space separated Bemo from Wooly. When a bullet tore into the marshal's outer left thigh, taking a chunk out as big as a beef steak, blood splattered Bemo's face, but surprisingly did not fill his eyes. Even more surprising, CB Wooly did not yet go down. Bemo watched as the marshal dropped the Colt from his right hand and pulled yet another one from the front of his trousers. Then Wooly fired once, twice and a third time to his front before dropping his right arm down along his side. At that point Bemo realized the Apache was no longer returning fire.

* * * *

CB Wooly did not grow bored with putting bullets in the Apache, nor had he finished the job. It existed a simple fact of the matter that his gun arm just refused to function a moment longer.

Wooly reached across his damaged body with his left hand and relieved the right hand of the pearl-handled Colt. Wooly carefully took one feeble step to his rear and then leaned back heavily upon the bullet riddled bar.

Laughing Billy looked to be only semi-conscious and squirmed at Wooly's feet. During the brief but hellacious battle, the Apache managed to move forward from the table at which he sat. He now rested on both knees, still upright, but swaying to and fro. His arms hung limp along his sides and the empty nickel-plated Smith and Wesson pistols dangled from his fingertips.

Nothing at the moment seemed easy for Wooly. Not breathing. Not standing. Not seeing. Not a damned thing. Except spouting blood. His mind seemed to have filled with a fog or smoke, slowing his thinking because only now did Stew Graybow come to mind. As quickly as he could, which wasn't quick at all, Wooly turned to look at the last place he'd seen the old man standing. Marvin Little looked to be frozen in place behind the bar, but Graybow was nowhere to be seen.

Wooly formed the question in his mind and tried to push it to his lips, but all that came out was a single word. "Graybow?"

"He ran out the back," answered Little, who sounded a hell of a lot further away from the spot he actually occupied.

Some time passed, maybe seconds, maybe minutes, before Little spoke again and this time sounded even further away. "I do believe you won this fight, Marshal Wooly."

CB did not feel certain of that fact, but he did feel certain of a sudden and powerful yearning to breathe fresh air and feel the light of day upon his skin. He let Clay Bardoe's pistol fall from his hand as he turned to face the bar in order to use it to work his way toward the swinging doors and the sunlight shining brightly beyond them. With palms down on the bar, he pushed and tugged and dragged himself toward the light.

Marvin Little rushed around the corner of the bar and offered a hand, but Wooly shook his head in defiance. He walked in on his own, and for reasons he did not fully understand, it seemed walking back out on his own might be the most important deed he ever accomplished. Once he reached the end of the bar, Wooly took deep and jagged breaths before pushing himself upright. Staggering, limping, stumbling, he made it to and out the swinging doors.

Thankfully, he located a column supporting the roof of the saloon's porch just outside the doors. Wooly grabbed it, wrapped his arms around it, and hung on for dear life. He did his best to breathe fresh air, but it just did not seem to fill his lungs. And the bright sunlight of late afternoon quickly started to dim as if evening approached much too quickly.

He hurt more now practically than he could bear. It felt as if he might be standing in the middle of a roaring fire. Wooly dropped his head and looked down at the blood pooling at his feet. He then heard behind him the heavy footsteps of booted feet pounding the boardwalk and coming quickly upon his back.

Wooly raised his head, but could not turn to look over his shoulder. Only able to look straight ahead, his blurry sight fell upon an image his mind could not explain. As he tried hard to focus his eyes for the sake of confirmation, the footsteps at his back drew closer, but he placed little concern in that fact. How could he care about anything else when to his front in the hard-packed dirt street stood a tall and slender man wearing a calf-length duster and light-colored Stetson with a Montana peak and a razor-sharp brim.

Because of distance and bodily damage, Wooly could not clearly see the face beneath the fine hat, nor did he need to. Still, boots pounded on the boardwalk at his back, sounding now only mere feet away as he summoned what little strength remained to call out to the figure in the street.

"Clay?"

A gloved hand slowly reached to tug at the brim of the Stetson as a greeting. A fleeting moment later the footsteps at Wooly's back ceased to fall and an angry voice filled the void.

"You should never have laid hands on me, you bastard!"

Three heavy blows landed in the middle of Wooly's back. Explosions reverberated through the fog or smoke in his head as the fire found its way into his guts. CB Wooly slid down the column, and rolled off the porch onto the dirt where his blood escaped in streams and fanned out about his body, darkening the place in the street where he lay.

CHAPTER NINETEEN

A promise made

A cook at the ranch house told Floyd Danner where to find the man he sought, and Danner found him right where the cook said he would be, branding calves in the north stock pins. Weary and aching from a three day's ride, Danner crawled off his Paint and up and over the corral fence. The man saw Danner coming, applied the branding iron to the downed calf's hide, and then stood and walked to meet Danner.

"Deputy Floyd Danner," Hound Olivo nodded in greeting and then offered a hand to be shook.

Danner shook the man's hand and took note of his sturdy grip. "I'm simply Floyd Danner now, Hound. I gave up being a lawman."

"I heard what happened back in Beaver City," Hound said with a sad looking shake of his head. "It's a damned pity."

"That it is, Hound. Ol' CB Wooly's been in the ground one month come yesterday. I carried him back to Stillwater and planted him next to Clay Bardoe. I thought he might like that."

Olivo nodded his head, but didn't seem to have words to put with the nod.

"Guess you've got to be wondering why I'm here," Danner said.

"It crossed my mind."

Danner didn't hesitate in telling his tale. "After that dirty back shooting bastard Stew Graybow put the final bullets in CB, he talked Marvin Little into helping him get Laughing Billy and the Apache on their horses. The three of them rode out, but not in the direction of Graybow's ranch. It was another two hours before I was allowed to give chase. I hate to admit to a man of your skills, but I wasn't even able to successfully track three sets of hoof prints and two men bleeding like a sieve. I lost all signs of them not thirty miles south and east of Beaver City. I spent another week looking for them, but came up empty handed. While I was away, the town folk hung Marvin Little off the side of the newly built jail."

"I hate to hear that," Olivo frowned. "Marvin wasn't a bad type."

"Nope. He was clearly the victim of very bad circumstances," Danner agreed before coming to the point. "Truth is, Hound, I need a man that can find men. I hear you're one of the best. Would you be willing to partner up with me to find Graybow and if they still be kicking, Laughing Billy and the Apache?"

Olivo sighed hard and turned to study the other cowboys doing what cowboys were intended to do. "What do you plan on doing if you find them?"

"If they'll allow me, I intend to hang them. If they don't, I intend to do my damnedest to butcher them where they stand."

Olivo sighed hard yet again. "Graybow was a fairly decent boss, but I can't stomach the things he's done."

It seemed obvious Olivo still had thinking to do and might cave to persuasion. "I can't afford to pay money, Hound. However, I now own CB's fine horse, Moonshine. The horse once belonged to Clay Bardoe. He's too big a horse for my squatty build, but I'll give him to you if you decide to throw in with me."

Olivo thought some more, nodded, and then did a little more thinking before removing his crusty hat and scratching at his short-cropped hair. "That's fair enough wages, I reckon. How soon we leave?"

Danner smiled in relief. "I'll come back for you. Presently, I have to visit a friend of a friend and keep a promise made."

Olivo looked back at the cowboys applying the red-hot brand to young hide. "Hell, Floyd, I might as well just ride on out with you now."

"The business I have to tend to ain't the pleasant type, Hound," Danner admitted.

"Is it any less pleasant than burning the flesh of baby cows, Floyd?" Olivo asked in a sincere manner.

"It involves killing a man," Danner confessed.

"I'm not sure any baby cow deserves being burned," Hound Olivo sighed, "but plenty of men deserve dying."

ACKNOWLEDGMENTS

Because these contributors are all so very dear to me and equally important to the outcome of this novel, I've listed them in alphabetical order.

To Kristen Remington, my administrative assistant, your technical skills and patience, make my life much easier to live. You are a gem.

To Henry P. (Pat) Scully of Scully Associates, many thanks for your remarkable cover design.

To SD Shelton, a very talented fellow author, I sincerely appreciate your guidance and inspiration.

To Jennifer Sims, Pat Scully's assistant, welcome to the team, and thanks for lending your creative eye for artwork.

Finally, to my tenacious editor, David Shupe, my novel couldn't be what it is without your superb editing skills. Without you, my spelling and grammatical flaws would be glaring. Many thanks.

ABOUT THE AUTHOR

Keith Remer is a retired Army colonel and an adjunct professor of history. He has to date written twelve novels and is the recipient of the *International Indy Book Award for Best of Fiction* for his novel, *The Hiding place of Thunder.*

Keith lives in rural Oklahoma City on his beloved horse ranch with any stray dog that comes along. He occasionally gets tossed from a horse but has survived in order to tell his tales.

Blood City is Book Two in *The Calamitous Breed Trilogy.*

Look for Book Three, *Reaping Hellfire,* coming in Spring of 2020

To connect with the author, visit his webpage keithremer.com, or his Facebook page @KeithRemerAuthor